VENDETTA

Borgo Press Books by ARDATH MAYHAR

The Absolutely Perfect Horse: A Novel of East Texas (with Marylois Dunn)
The Body in the Swamp: A Washington Shipp Mystery [Wash Shipp #2]
Carrots and Miggle: A Novel of East Texas
The Clarrington Heritage: A Gothic Tale of Terror
Closely Knit in Scarlatt: A Novel of Suspense
Crazy Quilt: The Best Short Stories of Ardath Mayhar
Deadly Memoir: A Novel of Suspense
Death in the Square: A Washington Shipp Mystery [Wash Shipp #1]
The Door in the Hill: A Tale of the Turnipins
The Dropouts: A Tale of Growing Up in East Texas
The Exiles of Damaria: A Novel of Fantasy
Feud at Sweetwater Creek: A Novel of the Old West
The Fugitives: A Tale of Prehistoric Times
The Heirs of Three Oaks: A Novel of the Old West
High Mountain Winter: A Novel of the Old West
How the Gods Wove in Kyrannon: Tales of the Triple Moons
Hunters of the Plains: A Novel of Prehistoric America
Island in the Lake: A Novel of Native America
Khi to Freedom: A Science Fiction Novel
The Lintons of Skillet Bend: A Novel of East Texas
Lone Runner: A Novel of the Old West
Lords of the Triple Moons: A Science Fantasy Novel: Tales of the Triple Moons
Makra Choria: A Novel of High Fantasy
Medicine Dream: Being the Further Adventures of Burr Henderson
Messengers in White: A Science Fantasy Novel
Monkey Station: A Novel of the Future (Macaque Cycle #1; with Ron Fortier)
People of the Mesa: A Novel of Native America
A Planet Called Heaven: A Science Fiction Novel
Prescription for Danger: A Novel of the Old West
Reflections; & Journey to an Ending: Collected Poems
A Road of Stars: A Fantasy of Life, Death, Love, and Art
Runes of the Lyre: A Science Fantasy Novel
The Saga of Grittel Sundotha: A Science Fantasy Novel
The Seekers of Shar-Nuhn: Tales of the Triple Moons
Shock Treatment: An Account of Granary's War: A Science Fiction Novel
Slewfoot Sally and the Flying Mule: Tall Tales from Cotton County, Texas
Soul-Singer of Tyrnos: A Fantasy Novel
Strange Doin's in the Pine Hills: Stories of Fantasy and Mystery in East Texas
Strange View from a Skewed Orbit: An Oddball Memoir
Through a Stone Wall: Lessons from Thirty Years of Writing
Timber Pirates: A Novel of East Texas (with Marylois Dunn)
Towers of the Earth: A Novel of Native America
Trail of the Seahawks: A Novel of the Future (Macaque Cycle #2; with R. Fortier)
The Tulpa: A Novel of Fantasy
Two-Moons and the Black Tower: A Novel of Fantasy
Vendetta: A Novel of the Old West
Warlock's Gift: Tales of the Triple Moons
The World Ends in Hickory Hollow: A Novel of the Future
A World of Weirdities: Tales to Shiver By

VENDETTA

A NOVEL OF THE OLD WEST

by

Ardath Mayhar

THE BORGO PRESS

An Imprint of Wildside Press LLC

MMIX

CONTENTS

VENDETTA

FOREWORD

I am a great admirer of aerialists, the Comanche, and hard-headed individualists. All of the above take part in this story that came about, oddly enough, as a result of seeing the first Indiana Jones movie. Something of the verve and adventurousness in that movie pushed a button, and off I went. The first scene was incredibly exciting, for I saw it in my mind as if it were a movie itself.

—Ardath Mayhar
Chireno, Texas
April 2009

Test the rigging!
Light the torches!
The performance is about to begin!

CHAPTER ONE

ARKANSAS, 1865

Torches flickered eerily, their light dancing in the heavy foliage of the thick forest surrounding the clearing. Only a handful of spectators sat in the flimsy stands erected for their use by the members of the tiny circus now engaged in its evening performance.

There were, Gian-Carlo calculated from his concealed position behind a wagon, about enough to feed the family for a couple of days. If they could manage to kill a wild pig for Leonello, the mangy lion, it might go further. There would be little coin in the till, but he could hear chickens squawking and a piglet grunting in the fenced area set aside for those who bartered their way into the show.

He shrugged his sequined cape behind his shoulders and straightened the tooled leather wristlets that had belonged to his grandfather, the first Gian-Carlo Gannelli. Grinning at the fretful mutter of the chickens, he waited to perform his part in the Gannelli Family Circus.

No tent hid the black sky. The poles and the rigging for the aerialists' performance formed dark webs picked out with red orange lines of reflected light. Torches flared around the clearing that he had helped to sawdust in the afternoon. Luckily the local sawmill exchanged its waste sawdust for tickets for the performance.

Now his mother's accordion and his father's violin were doing their joyous best with the March of the Comedians, while Cousin Barnabas flexed his gigantic muscles. A bear of a man, he stood in the ring, lifting the two ponies left to the circus.

These were tiny beasts, each now attached to a crossbar, their little hooves trotting in tempo, though they were suspended in the air. In the old days, before the War, it had been two horses that Cousin Barnabas lifted. But anything large enough to ride or to pull cannon or wagons had been commandeered by either the Rebs or the Yankees, as the circus fled from place to place, trying to avoid the war.

The spavined wagon horse paced wearily around the perimeter of the ring. On his back, Cousin Celie poised daintily on one foot, her still trim body describing a steely arabesque. As she neared her big husband, he lowered the ponies to stand on the sawdust and held out his hand. She stepped lightly onto his palm, letting the horse proceed without her.

Barnabas's arm did not dip, even slightly, beneath her not inconsiderable weight. He might have been holding a butterfly, so casually did he flip her up into the air. She somersaulted into a split on the ground before him. Then she rose, and they bowed together.

There was an enthusiastic spatter of applause. Mama and Papa Gannelli struck up a fanfare, and Johnny strode into the ring of torchlight, swirling his cape about him.

In the center of the ring he doffed his cape, letting it lie in a purple puddle at his feet, and bowed deeply. He moved to the nearer of the poles and began climbing the spidery rope of the ladder.

Light brightened around him as Cousin Barnabas cocked the reflectors behind the torches, casting their beams higher. Now they caught the high wire and the pair of trapezes suspended from a complex of wires and poles, which were all but out of sight in the darkness.

Behind him he could hear a louder burst of applause. He knew his Cousin Magda had made her appearance, in her skimpy costume. As he stepped onto the narrow platform, he felt the ladder twitch as she started up after him.

Papa, the first fanfare completed, was giving his spiel, but Johnny didn't listen. He had heard all that foolishness about the crowned heads of Europe and command performances for Napoleon himself.

Once, that had even been true. Before Old Nap had torn Europe apart and sent the Gannelli family fleeing to a safer continent, the circus had been a large one, with skilled performers from outside the family.

Johnny knew now that he would never see Europe, nor would Magda, for all her beauty and courage. He would be quite content if he and his group continued drawing enough audiences to keep themselves eating, in this war-ravaged South to which his grandfather had brought his circus. War seemed to pursue them relentlessly, no matter how they fled it.

The platform dipped gently beneath his feet, and he turned to Magda with a gallant gesture. Taking her hand, he bowed, feeling the thinness of her fingers, the calluses on her palm.

Hours of practice at acrobatics, knife throwing, bareback riding, lion taming (although poor Leonello had never in his long life had any chance to be wild) marked their hands. As well, they hunted wild pigs, birds, and raccoons. They fished in any promising stream, and they often poached from a farmyard, if it didn't seem even poorer than they.

Papa was ending his introduction. Johnny bowed to his cousin, to the spectators, and set the trapeze swinging. He was preparing to launch himself into space when something interrupted his concentration. An indrawn breath from dozens of lungs stopped him, and he let the correctly timed swing of the trapeze go by.

Peering down through the glare of the lamps, he saw the shapes of horses. Riders.

The crowd murmured, a sound instinct with fear. Papa came forward into the light, his fiddle in his hand, gesturing with Italian abandon.

"You interrupt our performance? I speet on you! The Emperor Napoleone, he interrupt the performance of the Family Gannelli. He send us from his shores to flee his wars. Now you! Why you do thees theeng?"

The Captain leading the group did not reply. In the center of the ring, he sat his sorrel, the torches showing the dust on his blue uniform. The audience stared at him and growled almost inaudibly at this conqueror in their midst.

"There he is!" shouted a soldier. Johnny shielded his eyes from the torchlight, finding at last two of the Yankees dragging forward the skinny youth they had taken on as a horse handler because he was starving to death. He had been tending the lamps on the farther side of the ring.

"Guerrilla!" came a voice to his ears. "Hang him! Damn bushwhacker—hang him!" The Captain waved his hand, and the men fell silent.

Turning on his horse to survey the rickety stands and the audience, the Captain said, "If you are wise, you will leave, now. You do not want to be here when I deal with these murderers of Union officers. Go!"

The whip-crack note in his voice sent them quickly and without protest toward their homes. Their night of magic had turned into a nightmare, in the space of a few heartbeats.

Once the last was out of sight, the Captain turned his attention to the Gannellis. Now they huddled together, fat Mama, her accordion clutched to her breast as if it might somehow protect her from this madman, Papa, flourishing his fiddle as if it were some exotic weapon. Cousin Celie and Barnabas clung together, Celie plastered against her giant husband like some vine clinging to a gigantic tree.

The officer's voice was harsh as he said, "Mountebanks! You have harbored a guerrilla, and I suspect that you, too, are guerrillas or spies. You!" he pointed to Papa. "Where did you find this scum? Why is he with you?"

At his motion, the two men pushed poor George forward. The boy was shaking so that he couldn't stand, and his sallow face was waxen with terror.

Papa Gannelli, his dark eyes afire with outrage, drew his portly figure up to its most dignified stature. He handed his violin to Barnabas and stepped forward.

"Thees is young boy, hurt and hungry. We, ourselfs, know well how it feels to be so. We take him with us. He can do work *we* do not need but that *he* need." He stared up at the man on the horse.

Johnny felt a surge of pride in his father. Even from so high up, he could see that Papa's face looked crumpled and old, totally unlike the round and rosy countenance he usually turned upon the world. He felt Magda's hand clamp hard onto his own in a spasm of sudden dread.

"Hmmmph!" the captain snorted. "Very thin. Under martial law, you are sentenced to hang, here and now. And as for those popinjays up there..."—He jerked his chin toward Johnny and Magda on their platform—"...They will be shot from their perch. Sergeant!"

Johnny saw the man kneel and steady his rifle. Even as he took aim, he could not believe that this could actually be happening. In a sane world, a just world, people who only tried to help and to entertain their fellows did not die because some madman on a horse commanded it.

Too late, he realized this was real. He was about to die. He was flinching backward against Magda before the slug plowed into his thigh.

Only Magda's quick reflexes saved him from a thirty-foot fall. She held him in an iron grip, as he sagged over the edges of the platform, and he could see that she was pale as milk as she stared down at the Captain below them.

"You can hang up there and hold him until you rot," the officer shouted to the girl. "There is not much you could do to stop what we're about to do, anyway. Watch the show, bitch!"

She kept staring down, though she never faltered as she clung to Johnny. He knew her arms must be screaming from the strain, but he watched, too, as the family was hustled to a bracing pole.

The sergeant flipped up a rope end. Then, under the direction of the Captain, he hanged Papa and Mama, along with their cousins Celie and Barnabas, who were Magda's parents. Before the ghastly struggles were done, Johnny was able to hold some of his own weight, although Magda hissed, "Stay dead! They'll shoot you again if you do not!"

As Papa, the last of them all, kicked into stillness, the officer turned again to stare upward. He was raising his hand, his gaze fixed upon the pair above him, when someone yelled, "That Reb has run!"

The officer wheeled his mount and began shouting orders. The ten men in his troop mounted quickly, and the entire group dashed off into the thickets around the clearing. Johnny could hear brush crashing and then the clatter of hooves on the rocky road leading toward town.

"Let us ask the Blessed Virgin to protect him," murmured his cousin.

"George is a country boy," Johnny muttered. "They'll never locate him in the woods."

They stayed as they were, muscles protesting the prolonged stress, until the last sound died away in the distance. Then Johnny reached for the edge of the platform, caught the sustaining ropes, and pulled himself upright.

Magda released her grip with difficulty and flexed her cramped hands until they worked again. "They had no time to burn the wagon," she whispered.

She swung around him and let herself down until her feet were securely on the rope ladder. "Can that leg bear your weight? I cannot carry you down, but I will brace from below as we go. Sit back against my shoulders. Hold tightly."

He cramped his fingers onto the rigging. Now the leg was like a lump of lead that had been thrust into a fire, but he managed to put his good foot onto the first crosspiece of the ladder. With great effort, he dragged the wounded leg off the platform. When it fell, limp, against the ropes, he hung on, letting nausea sweep through him.

Magda caught the bad leg and set the foot beside the other. Circling him with her arms, she hung onto the sides of the ladder. "Now, while you have the strength, we must go.

"They will come back, and when they do, we must be gone. Before we can go, we must tend your wound. I know they did not take the ponies, though they tied them, still harnessed to the beam, back in the trees."

Johnny grunted and held his weight with both hands, as he removed the good foot from the rung. The ladder, which was not meant to hold more than one person at a time, creaked and swayed and snapped, but he had achieved one step downward.

The pain was bearable. He repeated the process, with Magda bracing him from below and behind, keeping the bad leg from swinging.

It was a long way down. He was wringing wet by the time they stood again on the packed sawdust of the ring. With his cousin's help, he hopped toward the wagons, hidden behind a screen of hawthorn and brambles. If the Captain had seen them, he probably would have had them burned, and everything they needed for tending a wound was there. Injury was a constant companion of acrobats.

Yet Johnny found himself longing, more than anything else, for his case of throwing knives. He had never used firearms, but those razor-like blades were extensions of his hands, which now longed to use those deadly weapons against the man who had murdered his family.

CHAPTER TWO

Magda helped him to the space beside Papa's wagon and stretched him on one of the cots that had been set up outside in the shade of a big oak. She disappeared into the wagon and returned with Mama's emergency basket.

He fixed his eyes on the flame of the lamp she brought with her, knowing what must come now. He prided himself, afterward, that he had not grunted a protest when her knife probed his wound. He hadn't even moaned when she flooded whiskey into the long groove, once the slug was out.

She wound strips of bandage, layer after layer, knowing that they were going to stress the stitches she had made in his flesh. The pressure of the bandages was painful, yet somehow it was comforting, too. It lent strength to his leg, when he swung it to the ground.

Sitting, he found his head light. Much of his blood must now be soaked into the ground beneath that platform. Magda was looking into his eyes, assessing his condition as objectively as Mama used to do.

"I believe I can make it. I can move. But I must have my knives, and we will need clothing. We cannot run about the country dressed in purple tights. We should take food, too. Did the Yankees take all the produce in the pen?"

Magda bent to help him to his feet. "I will push, and you can get into the wagon. While you find what you need, I shall see about food from the other wagon. Not much was left in your Mama's stores except cornmeal and a bit of moldy bacon."

It wasn't easy, but at last Johnny found himself inside the vehicle that had been his home for all the years of his life. He thrust his head from the canvas cover and said, "See about the ponies. I can't walk, but one of those little fellows can carry me." He tried to grin, and she smiled, the quirk of her lip almost invisible in the flickering lamplight.

She had left another lamp lit inside the shelter. He found that if he used his leg, braced as it was with yards of bandage, as a sort of crutch, he could get about well enough, though the pain was so bad that he simply ignored it. Pain was the constant companion of aerialists.

Sitting on his father's humpbacked trunk, he could reach almost everything he needed. He stripped off the purple tights and bundled them into a knot, thinking that he would never see them again. Or the wagon or his parents.

The thought stung bitterly. He shook his head to clear away such distractions. He pulled on tough breeches, tugging them over his bandaged leg with difficulty. A heavy shirt and low-heeled work boots promised to serve his needs.

Almost, he took off those leather wristlets, but he recalled his grandfather's words. "These, they are geeft, Gian-Carlo, from the Queen of Napoli. See how soft the leather? How nice the tooling? They have even gems, though not showy. Very small, very refined. They weel be yours, Grandson, on the day you go aloft for your first perforr-mance!"

No, he would not leave behind the gift of the Queen of Naples for some Yankee to paw over. He pulled his cuffs down over the wristlets and looked about him.

Clothes for Magda were already in a bundle, with extras for both. Coats. Though it was now spring, there was no certainty that winter would find them able to procure more. Blankets were rolled into packs about the food, the clothing.

The knife case, fine leather lined with silk, had gone into one of those rolls, but the knives themselves disappeared into his clothing. Each slender shaft of steel fitted into its own pocket or loop. When he had finished, no one could have guessed that he was armed with a dozen bits of instant death.

When Magda returned, she was leading the ponies, both still attached to the connecting beam. On the back of the smaller there were bundles containing lumps that Johnny suspected were potatoes and squash and beans. No soldier ever passed up a chicken or a pig, but vegetables didn't make a noise to betray their presence.

"I'm glad potatoes don't squawk," he said. He hobbled about, helping Magda load their few belongings onto the pony. They used some spare rigging from the bareback act as pack-straps, and a small saddle under the wagon seat went onto the larger animal.

"By the time he gets too weary to carry me, I will be unable to ride any longer, anyway," Johnny said. He leaned on the pony, feeling the stocky strength of the beast. "But they are much stronger than they look."

Magda came down from the wagon after changing into tough clothing. She now looked like a boy, her glorious mane of black hair cut short with Mama's big scissors. A loose shirt hid the curves that would have betrayed her, and Johnny made a mental note to remind her not to bump into anyone. Steely as her muscles might be, she still had that unique softness that belonged to women.

"We'd better go." His voice quivered, and his hand lingered on the weathered wood of the wagon, the only home he had ever known. "I hate to leave things like this. I hate to leave our people unburied. Many things I hate!"

Now his voice was grim, the quaver gone. "I know," said his cousin. "Let us bring them to the wagon on the pony. We shall burn them, wagon and all. There will be nothing left for those filthy beasts to handle or to steal."

It was insane. The troop might be back any moment, but the pair were determined. Johnny knew that he would never be at rest in his own spirit if he did not do this last service for those he loved.

The pony carried two at a time, once he got over snorting and stamping with alarm at the smell of death clinging to them. When the four were laid out on the wagon's floor, rather crowded together, but that had been true as much in their lives as in their deaths, Magda poured over them the last of the lamp oil.

Johnny flung the lamp into the opening and stood with Magda, watching the blaze take hold. Tears streamed down their faces as the canvas crackled and flared, the old wood popped and groaned.

He had never understood the horror of these southern Americans at the thought of weeping. For them, only women cried, but Italians wept when they were happy or sad, angry or joyful. It was a tremendous relief for the soul.

He raised both hands in a sort of salute. "Goodbye, Mama, Papa, Cousin Barnabas, Cousin Celie. We have done our best by you." He stared into the flames, feeling his head reel with blood-loss and the beginning of fever.

"Now we shall avenge you." Magda stared at him, her expression strange in the glare of the burning wagon. The smell of flesh cooking came to Johnny's nostrils, and he retched.

His cousin turned and caught him, pushing him onto the pony. Then she led her strange caravan into the night-bound forest.

Johnny closed his eyes against his own giddiness. The pony's choppy gait almost dislodged him, and he clung to the cropped mane, hooking his good leg into the straps to help stabilize himself as they hurried through the wood.

For a very long while he could, when he opened his eyes, still see flecks of red light against tree trunks and leaves. After a time, they moved past the range of the firelight, and the blackness closed about them.

"Can you keep from going in circles?" he asked, coming to himself in a rare moment of lucidity.

Magda didn't answer, and before he could repeat the question he was dissolved again into the mist of pain and fever that held him. But someplace inside he knew that she read the stars as others read books. Up there beyond the treetops, the sky was clear, and she was taking note of their positions every time she caught a patch of sky among the tangled branches.

If it could be done, his cousin would lead them to safety.

CHAPTER THREE

Before dawn, Magda called a halt. Johnny, rousing from his dream of pain and fever, saw that she had found a sheltered spot between a pair of gray boulders.

When she helped him off the pony, he thought for a moment that he would fall. Magda held fast, however, and the pony stood under his leaning weight until he could get his balance again. Then, half sitting on a smaller rock, Johnny helped his cousin hobble the ponies before she turned them to graze in the meadow clearing that edged a bank of the small stream she had followed northward.

Behind them the ground sloped upward sharply. Beyond the creek the forest was thick and tangled. This little pocket of clearing would have to do, for neither he nor the pony could go farther.

It was early yet, too early to stop, with those angry troopers behind them, but there was no alternative. Magda made it clear that a day of rest might make the difference between his healing or his death.

He remembered little of the argument later, for he was still groggy and disoriented with blood loss. She managed to help him into the shade, though he recalled that she had to eject an angry copperhead from its daytime rest.

They crawled into the long crevice running back between the big rocks, and Johnny slept. When he woke, Magda was looking about her alertly.

"It's just too peaceful," she said. "I don't trust it. By now I know the Yankees have gone back to the camp and found us gone. They know you weren't dead and that we are in the forest.

"That idiot did not take me seriously at all, which is as well or we both would have been shot and fallen to our deaths. Sometimes it is an advantage to be considered a weak fool. But that officer will have men trailing us. And at night I could not see well enough to cover the back trail."

"No help for it," Johnny managed to mumble, though even his tongue felt exhausted. "Mus' sleep."

She dug in her pack and found the bottle of laudanum that Mama kept for emergencies. When he had taken a dose of that, Gannelli was out for a long time.

A shot woke him. He rolled over and looked for Magda. She stood in the shelter of the rocks, staring upward the way they had come, examining the forest, the long slants of light from the setting sun, the shadows that now were merging into dimness.

Sighing, Johnny pulled himself up to sit. She turned toward him, but there came a crack from the upland wood. A horse whickered, and in a flash she slipped from the crevice in which she had stood and signaled with finger clicks to the ponies.

Trained to respond to such signals, the pair left their grazing and pranced to her side. Neither whinnied in reply to the horse in the wood as she led them around the boulders to another sheltered cranny, just large enough for the two of them.

Johnny, lying in the cave-like opening between his boulders, knew that she was tightening their harness, making certain their loads were replaced and secured. If they had to run again, they would be ready.

When she crawled into the crevice, Johnny squeezed to one side. "Get behind me," he whispered. "There is a pile of stones back there where part of the rock fell. If I miss, you may need them for ammunition.

There was a sound of hooves on grass and pebbles. Three horses...Johnny quirked a brow at Magda, and she nodded.

"They've got to be around here," said a voice that was twanged with the sharp R's of the north. "That man was hard hit. I could tell by the way he fell, and that little woman couldn't possibly be much help to him. If we'd shot those ponies, they never could have got away.

"You look over by the brook, Marvin. I'll check that patch of brush."

A third voice spoke, so near the boulders that Johnny jumped, startled. "Look here, sergeant. There's a cave back here in this pile of rock. They could be holed inside there."

Johnny lifted his hands and gave them a slight shake. Two blades appeared in his fingers, and he wiggled as well as he could into a tight crouch against the wall.

Magda squeezed against the other wall, almost touching his back with her elbow. He could hear her arranging her pile of stones conveniently.

"You be careful," came the first voice. "There might be snakes in there—never saw such country for nasty varmints. Marvin, you come over here and cover us. Ben, you look inside, but be careful."

It was dark inside the narrow crevice. The man's bulk blocked off what light there was still in the clearing, as he hunkered down to peer into the darkness. Johnny knew that after the light outside the interior must seem totally black.

"Sarge," said Ben, "I don't think there's a soul in here. It's dark as the inside of a bear."

"Make certain," the sergeant said, and his shadow, coming close behind the other man, obscured the interior even more. "You crowd over and let me look. I have eyes like an eagle."

Before either could move, there came two swift flickers of bright metal in the darkness of the little cave. Both quenched themselves in the bodies at the mouth of the opening; the sergeant and the private fell forward into the darkness, dying without another word.

Magda sighed. "Just one more," came her words, the merest breath in his ear. "Perhaps I can lure him into the cave."

"Yes." He waited, tense with expectation. "Oh!" she shrieked so suddenly that even he was startled. "You're hurting me! Let me go! He is not here—you can see that. He died, and I put him into the wagon with the others."

Hurried steps approached the cave. "Need any help, Sarge?" The third man, Marvin, bent to look into the opening.

Before he could realize that the boots of his companions were all he could see, and those were suspiciously still, a stone struck him squarely in the forehead, embedding itself like a third eye. At the same moment, another knife punctured this throat. "Arrgh!" he said. Then he was dead.

"That Captain will search for them," Johnny said. "We must be gone before they find them unless, of course, they cannot be found."

Magda slipped past him and stood on the grass outside the opening. "Their horses are over beside the brook. Be still for a moment. I can catch them, if nothing startles them."

He knew she could—she was a wonder with animals of all kinds, and Leonello was more like her kitten than an African lion. He busied himself with dragging the three limp bodies deeper into the cranny. His leg made that difficult, for now it was swollen, throbbing violently, but he managed it.

He crammed them into the very back of the space and brought down more of the rotten stone on top of them. From outside, the little tunnel looked empty; even when he lit a candle stub and examined it carefully, he found only traces of blood on the dusty floor. Handfuls of additional dust covered that well.

When Magda returned with the horses and the ponies, she looked carefully and found his work passable. "Nobody will ever suspect they were here at all. I have brushed out the tracks of the horses coming in, and I shall do it again going out of this spot.

"But what about the Army gear on these horses?"

Johnny thought for a moment, rocking gently to ease the pain that now was moving up his hip and into his back.

"Dump everything into the stream where it bends. There should be a deep hole there. Roll their weapons into our blankets, and put the small saddle from the pony onto one of the horses.

"If we let out the girth, it should fit. We don't want any McLellan saddle giving us away, but I am going to need stirrups for a time. You can make do with a blanket?"

Without speaking, which was one of her most endearing traits, Magda packed everything efficiently onto the horses, using one as a pack animal. When she was done, she looked at the ponies.

"What about them? They have been with our family for years, yet they are slower. We cannot take them, do you think? They couldn't keep up with these long-legged beasts, but how I hate leaving them behind!"

"We can let them follow us for a time, on the back trail. Then we can drive them into the woods. I hate it, but what else can we do?"

"Along our back trail?" She stared at him, her eyes widening. "We are going back?"

Johnny nodded. "They expect us to run. I am hurt, but I am not out of it. Not yet. Now, while I am able, I intend to hunt them. There are only seven left, besides that Captain." He spat the last word as if it tasted bitter.

Magda's laugh had an edge of hysteria. "Gian-Carlo Gannelli, the great warrior! I never knew you were so fierce, Johnny. Yet you are correct. It is not what they will expect us to do.

"If they catch us, we will be no more dead than if we attack them and die. They would give us no more chance for life than they did your parents and mine."

Now it was fully dark in the forest, though the sky still held traces of bright cloud. After Magda disposed of the Army gear, she helped him to mount, although there was a very bad moment when his upper thigh had to take a bit of weight. He thought for an instant that he might faint.

He settled himself before speaking. "I'll have to work from horseback, Mag. There will be no getting up and down for me, I know now. Not until this thing heals. So you will need to do the scouting and all the footwork. All right?"

"And who is the one who catches wood doves with her two hands?" she asked sweetly. "I am quieter in the forest than you, *caro mio*. Lead on, if you can find your direction. I will follow, leading the pack horse."

Johnny led the small procession, pausing while Magda felt for tracks and brushed out any her sensitive fingers found. As they wound through the trees, he felt the location of the camp as if it were a warm spot on his face, drawing him toward the revenge those Yankees had earned.

He stopped after a time, and let Magda haze the ponies away into the dark wood. Then they both pushed the horses as fast as Johnny could bear to ride. Soon there was no sound of any hooves other than the heavy ones of their mounts and the pack horse.

At last Magda made him halt. "I know you must be bleeding again," she said. "Let me check the dressings, for if you lose too much blood you will not be able to lift a knife, far less to throw one."

She fumbled in the darkness. There came the click of flint and steel, and a flame grew where she knelt beside her tinderbox. She lit the candle from that, quenched it thoroughly, and came to examine the bandaged leg.

A telltale thread of blood showed through the thick layerings of bandage. "Sit still," she said, as he moved to dismount. "I can dress it from here, if you help me to lift the leg. Hold on tight for a moment."

She dolloped alcohol into the wound and packed it with cotton wool from Mama's medical stores. Then she wound it again with strips of clean cotton. "That should hold you together until we find a place where you can rest. Or do you intend to take on the Yankee army tonight?" She stared up, her dark eyes quizzical in the candlelight.

"Perhaps not tonight," he said through gritted teeth. He felt as if he had been in the hands of torturers. "I think that I must rest soon. My head is light, going round and round."

"Um-hmmm," she said. "I thought so. Now, those Yankees will not look for us in the darkness. As yet they do not know those behind us are missing. Probably, they had orders not to return without us, so it may be some time before the Captain becomes alarmed.

"Tomorrow he may begin to wonder, but tonight we should be able to sleep with some safety. If we can find a sheltered spot in which to lie down." She glanced about her. Then she smiled.

"Ahead there is a bend in the path to miss a very large oak. I recall a thicket, off to the right, though now it will be the left. We can hide there for hours, but we must move early. It is best to attack before dawn, do you not agree?"

The thicket was there. Some fifteen minutes later, he found himself flat on a blanket while Magda tethered the horses, easing their bits so they could crop brush tops around them. When she was done, she returned and rolled them both in the same cocoon of blankets, which smelled faintly of horse.

"You remember how they used to lay me on horse blankets, when I was tiny, to watch the family rehearse?" she murmured. "I have always loved the smell of horses."

Johnny didn't answer. The memory of their mutual past was still too painful to face, and in self defense he drifted off to sleep, away from the pounding in his leg.

CHAPTER FOUR

A mockingbird woke him very early. The moon was just past zenith, and even in the thick forest slender pencils of light struck through the new leaves in places. One of those lay in a puddle on the blanket covering Johnny. He fumbled in his pocket and brought out his father's big silver watch, the only thing he had taken from his parents' bodies except for his mother's wedding ring.

By the uncertain light, he scanned the face, making the hour three-thirty. He nudged Magda. "*Cara!* It is time."

"Mama, no! S'too early!" she murmured. "Can't see to practice."

"Shhh! Magda, it's time to go. We must defeat the Grand Army of the Republic today. Have you forgotten that?"

"Mmmm Johnny? Oh!" Her eyes opened, and she sat up, joggling his leg as she moved.

"Ouch! Be careful, *Cara!*" She shivered and stretched before rising to her feet.

"Are you able to move? I shall get the blankets rolled, if you can."

He moved his leg, and the devil and all his imps grabbed it with red-hot pincers, doing their worst. "Remind me to stop at the first church we find and go to confession," he said.

He forced the tortured limb to move, pushing it with his uninjured knee. "I now have a small idea of how Hell must feel, and I think that I do not want a closer acquaintance."

Magda chuckled. "Your Mama would be happy to hear you say that. How often did she try to drag you to church, when we could find Catholics, only to have you wiggle out of going? If this awful thing manages to bring you to heaven at last, she will consider it, I am certain, well worth her own suffering."

Johnny caught a slender pine sapling and hauled himself upright, as Magda folded the blankets and rolled the packs. He balanced there, holding now to two tree trunks, trying to straighten the wounded leg. After some effort, he succeeded.

Moving it as much as possible, he said, "You have kept it so full of alcohol that I feel it won't infect. Once it is in operation again, I probably will forget about going to that church."

She grunted, fastening the strings about the blanket-rolls. "Just as I thought. Ah, well, I am no better than you. Our Mamas spent many an hour on their knees, pleading with God on our behalf. You would suppose that would make us devout. But perhaps we are right, after all, and all that is useless."

Johnny hobbled toward the picketed horses, using a broken off stub of branch as a crutch. "I will never forget Grandfather's tale about the priest in France who sold those fleeing from the Revolution, when they took sanctuary in his church. He made a fortune from that, according to the old story. I could never bring myself to trust one, after that."

Magda came behind, lugging the awkward rolls. She saddled his horse and blanketed her own, tying the supplies again to the pack animal.

"Come now. If we must move at such an ungodly hour, let's be going. My question is this: *where* are we going?"

"Back to the circus." Johnny hauled himself painfully onto the back of his mount, and Magda came to put his foot in the stirrup. "I feel they may have camped there for the night, so the searchers would know where to return, once they caught us. And the Captain may even think that we will return there when we think it is safe. And so we will, safe or not, but not as they expect us to."

They did not move directly toward the camp along the stream, as they had left it. Cutting across the loops and bends, they kept the creek in sight as a guide, for it was often marked by the glint of its waters in the moonlight. Magda, watching the stars, still, paused at last and waited for Johnny to come up with her.

"We are near now," she whispered, and Johnny knew that she was correct. "But I just remembered Leonello has not been fed or watered in many hours. Caged, he will starve. What can we do? He has been our friend since he was a cub, and we cannot leave him in this way."

Johnny grinned, feeling it as a grimace that was almost painful. "His cage was in the thicket not too far from the wagon. We put him in the shade, and unless he has been restless and made noise, they may not have found him. He sleeps most of the time now, anyway. I filled his water tank just before the show began, so he should not be upset. Perhaps he can help us avenge his old friends. Can you get to him without letting anyone see or hear you?"

Magda grunted, and they moved forward slowly, keeping to the leaf-strewn path they had found. After a few minutes, Johnny drew rein and nodded toward the left. "They are there, in the old camp. Can't you smell them? If you can creep near enough to spy out their disposition, I will think about what to do."

Magda slid off her horse and dissolved into the brush without a sound. Johnny, listening to the early morning calls of the birds, the burbling of the stream, found his mind empty. No inspiration was there, though he had found his imagination teeming with ideas as they rode.

Before he found a workable plan, Magda was back. "Leonello is in his cage asleep. There is no sign that they found him, for the bushes are thick and the cage wagon doesn't show from the rest of the camp."

She came closer, her whisper softening. "They camped in the ring, on the sawdust. There is a mound beside the spot where the wagons burned; they must have buried whatever...was left." He heard her swallow hard.

"Three men are on guard, one just down there beside the stream, one on the approach from the road, and one on the trail going up into the heights to the east. They are awake and alert. They didn't see me." She sounded smug.

"Did you open the cage?"

"Yes. I got inside and woke the old sluggard. I told him what we need for him to do as well. Mama always insisted that he cannot understand what I say, but he looks as if he does, and this was no exception. We can take care of the guard on this side while he makes up his mind to do what I asked him."

Johnny nodded, feeling for his knives. "Do you want a knife or two?"

"That might be best. I am not quite as skilled as you, but they are silent. I can manage, and we cannot afford a shot. Not yet." She reached for the slivers of steel that he handed down.

"You can pin a flea to a cat hair without skinning the cat! Don't try to sound modest. Godspeed, Cara!" He watched as she eased through the early morning dimness into the trees.

After a few moments, she wavered into view again and came near, to whisper, "Can you make him come this way? I can't get near, as he is positioned."

Johnny bent in the saddle and breathed, "Hand me two pebbles from the stream."

She did and was gone again. He waited sixty seconds, measured by his own pulse. Then he clicked the pebbles together, the sound sharp in the cool morning air. Once more, and again, at irregular intervals. It was an odd sound, but not menacing.

A picket should investigate such a matter without sounding an alarm. They were lucky, for this one did just that.

Stepping cautiously out of the nest of huckleberry bushes that topped the ridge just above the creek, the man came into sight. There came a sudden flash of silver in the dawnlight, and the picket went down without more than a muffled gurgle.

The mockingbird, still welcoming the new day, sang energetically in the walnut tree over the creek. There was no other sound at all.

Johnny willed Magda to take the trooper's gun. But he knew his cousin, and she stooped, leaving the shelter of the bushes, and caught up the rifle he had dropped. Laying it aside, she unbuckled his belt and retrieved the revolver as well. Rummaging for a moment, she came up with ammunition for both weapons.

Then she removed the knife from his left eye and wiped it on his shirt before returning it to the sheath on her own belt.

As she straightened and turned toward Johnny, a soul-shattering roar boomed through the waking wood. Magda gave a startled leap and gained her cousin's side.

"Leonello!" she gasped, holding to the stirrup. "But how did he know to roar so? He has never before in all his life sounded like a real lion!"

"You said that he understood you," Johnny said. "Perhaps he did. Now let us go and attend to these pitiless murderers of our people."

Magda swung onto her own mount, secure as an Indian on the blanket saddle. As they wheeled their horses, bedlam broke loose beyond the screen of trees and brush.

She giggled. "I cut the picket ropes, too. The horses are all loose, and that roar is sending them mad. It is time, indeed, Gian-Carlo, to visit this Captain who hanged our parents."

CHAPTER FIVE

Johnny drew a long breath, bracing himself against the agony that movement was going to bring. Then he kicked his good heel into the horse's flank, and the two of them thundered through the barrier of trees and bushes, bursting into the camp.

Men were scrambling out of blankets, running in socked feet after the mounts that were disappearing in all directions into the forest. The Captain, standing in the middle of the chaos, was firing his revolver into the air to gain attention, but he was only adding to the confusion.

Johnny was no marksman, but at such close range it was impossible to miss with the rifle he had taken from the dead sergeant. Behind him, Magda was using a pistol. Two men fell before the Captain realized that he was being attacked and turned toward them.

He leveled his own revolver, but before he could fire Johnny flipped a knife, which drew a scarlet line across his knuckles. The gun dropped into the pine straw at his feet, and he grabbed his wrist with his left hand.

Magda kneed her mount close and covered him with her pistol, while Johnny rode up to block the view from any troopers who might look toward their officer. He stared down into puzzled eyes. The man evidently had no idea who they might be.

That was not at all surprising. They had been high up, lit only by wavering torchlight, wearing purple tights. The platform, Johnny had noticed as he came into the ring, still swayed forlornly from its braces, and recalling what had been done here, he found his temples pounding.

Magda's laugh called him back to the present, although the shape of the Captain seemed to shimmer amid tides of fever. "He doesn't recognize us, Johnny. He shot you and he hanged our family, but he doesn't even know us. That is funny, is it not?"

Johnny grinned, feeling no amusement. "The next time we meet, he will have no doubt. This will be the thing he will recognize." He pulled back the cuff of his shirt, and the leather wristlet gleamed in the dim light of dawn.

The Captain seemed to shrink, his straight back losing a trace of its starchiness. He opened his mouth to speak, but a shattering roar interrupted him. Leonello was moving through the wood toward the mountain on the east.

Johnny shivered, the fever now raging in his blood. "Mountebanks, are we? Scum for the hanging? People with foreign names and foreign ways cluttering up the landscape? Well, *figlio mio*, we are something more than that.

"You have killed our world. Our lives revolved around our tiny circus and the members of our family. Now I am about to kill your world. Or as much as we can catch." He nodded to Magda, who reversed her handgun and hit the man expertly behind the ear.

The Captain went down like a sack of sand. Under Johnny's direction, Magda dragged him over to the nearest tree and bound him securely to the trunk. Then she removed his trousers and tied them about his neck by the legs. Johnny laughed, then, rocking in the saddle, ignoring the flashes of pain running the length of his leg.

Magda touched his ankle, bringing him back to himself again. Together, they hunted the troopers through the trees. They had killed half the complement already, counting the three who had hunted them. Three lay dead in the ring. Only four remained, and they were easy to find, crashing through the timber after their mounts.

Once they had disposed of all his men, the Gannellis returned to the Captain. Johnny shot him through the calves of both legs, without hitting the bone. He would recover to suffer again, if they could manage that. Killing him now would be too easy. He had to lose everything before he lost his life.

They searched for Leonello, but there was no trace of the lion. He had evidently headed for the heavy forest.

"He will starve," Magda said, her tone mournful. "He has lived all his life in a cage, with people to feed him."

Johnny stared up into the sunlit heights above them. "Perhaps it is better so. Everything should be free at least once in its life. He will have the spring and the summer to learn to hunt for himself. If he can learn to roar, so late in his life, he can probably learn to catch rabbits and opossums.

"The winters here are harsh, but he might well live for years, a free lion in the Arkansas forest. The people will find it frightening, and yet I think they will also find it exciting as well. That is a wonderful thought, do you not agree?"

Magda's smile was shaky. "True. Even Leonello may have a chance to be a predator, to be truly the beast he was born to be. I had not thought of that."

They checked the mound beside the burned wagons. On a gum tree leaning over the spot, Magda carved a single word: GANNELLI. Then she checked over the gear of the dead troopers, taking what ammunition, food supplies, and blankets she thought they might need.

A few horses had begun to wander back by the time she was done, and Johnny hazed them into the trees again. Army mounts were branded, and he didn't want any more than the three they had.

When everything was done, they moved back toward the tree to which their victim was tied. The Captain's eyelids fluttered open. His gaze fixed upon Johnny, and his lips pulled back in a grimace, as he realized his predicament.

Ridicule, demotion, those were the things awaiting an officer who lost his entire command, along with his dignity, to this sort of reprisal. He knew it, Johnny saw that in his eyes. What he did not yet understand was that this was only the first indignity the Gannellis intended to visit upon the bastard, if they lived to carry the vendetta further.

They pushed through more bushes, moving along the stream toward the south. As they went, the two ponies burst out of a thicket and joined them, whickering with joy. Johnny, reeling in his saddle, looked toward Magda.

She was grinning. "I won't drive them away. They are all we have left of our family, and if they can keep up, why not let them come along? They are clever, full of unusual tricks that few ponies have ever been taught. They may be very convenient. We are, I think, now at war with the United States of America?"

Johnny was shocked into alertness for a moment. "I had not considered that. But it is true every instant of that man's life, I want him to listen for our voices and our footsteps. Being an officer and a 'gentleman,' he will be compelled to tell his superiors who we are, instead of claiming that he was attacked by a large band of guerrillas.

"They will put a price on our heads. They will hunt for us as they did for poor George. We are, indeed, at war." It was a sobering notion, and for a moment it kept him from drifting into his fever dream again.

Magda moved her horse close beside him and held him straight in the saddle. "For now you must rest and find a secure place to be quiet while your wounds heal. You are going to be too sick and feverish to travel. We are not far from the Red River crossing into Texas. What would take our wagons a week to do, stopping to perform from time to time, can be done by these horses in a day and a night, if you can hold on that long." She stared at him, assessing his condition.

"They will look for us in Arkansas. If we are to the south, in Texas, they may fail to look there for us until we have time to move farther. Grandfather used to say that the military mind is methodical. Think in unusual patterns, and you can outwit it every time."

"Wise Mag," said Johnny. "There is a lot of country to the southwest, and we could lose ourselves there, with luck. We can be secure for as long as we need, and once I am able again, I am certain that there will be Yankee troops to inconvenience."

Her black eyes were fixed on his face. "First we must get to the river and into Texas. I can see the fever in your eyes, Gian-Carlo. I refuse to carry your corpse westward. If you wish to go, it must be as a living man."

She wheeled her horse and stared up at the sun. "The stream runs directly into the river. Papa was wishing we could follow it, instead of winding along the road, for it is much more direct as a route. We can cut through on horseback. Come now."

He glanced over his shoulder toward the camp, now invisible behind the thick growth. He had insisted that Magda lay the caps and rifles of the dead Yankees on the mound that was the grave of their people. Now he wondered if it had been the fever which made that seem so important.

With a sigh, he turned his own horse, cursed softly as the leg reacted to the movement, and followed his cousin along the path edging the stream. He would hang on until they crossed the river. Then who knew?

* * * * * * *

It was a grueling journey. More than once, Johnny had to pull up before time to rest the horses, simply because his leg became unbearable. Each time, Magda inspected the bandages, and once or twice she stripped off the blood-soaked cloth and washed the wound again with whiskey. Whether the treatment or the relief from the extra pain it caused was the reason, after such pauses Johnny was able to go on more easily for quite a long while.

They made progress, under Magda's grim determination, and soon they were in the low country edging the river. As it was spring, there was water everywhere. Marshes impeded them, and early mosquitoes began zinging in their ears. Yet at last Johnny found himself staring at the mud-red channel, its wide expanse broken by sandbars, which were also red.

The river was higher than usual, but they found a shallower spot and used the sandbars as a guide as they rode into the stream. Johnny found the flow of cool water about his leg a comfort, as his mount began swimming.

The ponies stood on the shore behind, whinnying frantically as the larger beasts moved across the stream. They galloped up and down, snorting, and at last they plunged in and followed their old friends onto the soil of Texas.

Indignant as they seemed, they had come as quickly as the longer-legged animals, and Johnny knew that they would be able to keep up, no matter how far the odd group traveled. The question in his mind was his own ability to go any farther at all.

CHAPTER SIX

They had to find higher ground out of the marshy land, and, they hoped, away from the worst of the mosquitoes. Although he could see nothing, for it was night again, Johnny realized that he was hearing the thud of solid ground beneath the hooves of the horses. There seemed to be fewer insects, although the cries of frogs and crickets were loud in his ears.

"Johnny!" That was Magda, her voice rousing him from a grim dream. "I have found a ridge. It is as good as we will get in the dark. You can get down now. I have blankets already spread so you may lie down."

Her hands tugged at him, but he hardly understood what she said. The combination of fever and pain had carried him far away, into a country inhabited by lions and clowns, by Mama and Papa and the joyful circus of his youth. But at last he realized what she wanted, and he fell off into her arms, carrying them both to the ground.

The shock of anguish brought him to his senses. He inched backward to lean against the trunk of a small tree, while his cousin built a fire of brush and twigs. By its light she rubbed down all the animals and turned them loose, the army mounts hobbled, to graze on the spring grass.

They were, indeed, on a ridge, and early dawn was turning the meadow between it and the marshes gray with its tenuous light. As the horses plodded away, their teeth tearing succulent clumps of grass, Magda set the coffee pot on the coals and dragged up dead branches from beyond the ridge.

Johnny managed to drink a bit of coffee, but he wasn't able to eat more than a bite of her beans and bread. At last Magda turned and motioned for him to lie flat on the blankets. Johnny braced his hands against the tree as she took out her medicine basket.

Cutting away the infected tissue, she again doused his wound with alcohol, stitched the long groove with Mama's needle and thread, and dosed him with Mama's laudanum. Though he had bitten his tongue badly as she worked, the bitter stuff put him out entirely.

They remained there for three days and nights. Johnny roused to sip medicine or herb tea or broth that tasted like rabbit. His cousin, left to her own devices in wild country, was efficient at bringing down small game.

He roused fully in the evening of the third day, feeling weak and light in the bone. His leg was no longer a blaze of agony, although when he moved there was a long ache down his thigh.

There was a pot taken from the Yankees, Johnny decided, simmering over a small fire, held by a tripod. Magda squatted by the coals, stirring from time to time with Mama's big horn spoon. The smell made Johnny's gut growl with hunger, and he struggled to sit straight.

At once, his cousin was beside him, helping him to his feet. She had cut saplings to make crutches, padding the tops with strips of blanket, and she assisted him as he moved into the bushes to relieve himself. When he returned, she grinned.

"I have been doing all that for you for days now. Why so shy, *Caro*?"

To his disgust, Johnny felt himself blushing, but he ignored her teasing and hobbled with some difficulty to the fire. They had grown up together, and such shyness had come only after they were older.

She handed him a bowl of rabbit stew, flavored with wild greens and wild onions, and he leaned against the tree to eat. He could feel the food moving into his body, filling his stomach, strengthening him.

When he slept again, it was with total relaxation. And when Magda woke him in the dawn, he knew he could now ride. Not easily or well, but he was on the mend.

Leaving their ridge, they rode across gently rolling country with hills crowned with stands of big timber. The grass growing in the meadows was already up to their knees as they sat their horses, and the beasts took an occasional bite as they passed through the rank growth.

Grazing at night, the animals began getting fat, and Johnny, fed on the bounty of stolen Yankee foodstuffs, began to feel stronger. They moved more quickly, traveling south and west, deeper into Texas.

That brought them to the first farm they had seen. They would have circled wide to avoid it, if there had not been a bank of threatening cloud stretching up the sky as a boiling darkness across the northwest. The morning turned dark blue, and gusts of wind rippled the grass and the trees.

A storm was on its way, and it was coming fast. The low house toward which they rode was quite large, with a railed enclosure at the rear in which several sheds and the foundation of a barn had been built. Made of logs and heavy timbers, the buildings seemed solid enough to withstand the coming wind.

"You don't need to get wet," said Magda. "You'd get pneumonia, without a doubt. Let's take the chance and ask for shelter. We can't avoid people forever."

As much as he hated to risk it, Johnny knew that she was right. "Just pray that these are not people who have dealings with Yankee troops," he muttered, as they reined up in the front yard, which was scraped dirt with round flowerbeds showing the promise of color to come.

Four dogs bounded around the house and began barking with all their might. The front door opened, and a flood of children poured out onto the porch, followed by a very large lady whose most noticeable feature, at the moment, was a double-barreled shotgun, cocked and ready for instant use.

"Buenos días," she said, her black eyes examining every aspect of both riders and horses. She seemed to think that her conversational duties were completed with the greeting, and there came a long pause.

"¿Habla usted Inglés?" asked Magda, who had lived for a time, as a child, with her Spanish grandmother.

The woman relaxed a bit. *"Sí. Un poco.* What you want? What are you called?"

Johnny shot a warning glance at his cousin before replying, "I am Johnny Gann. This is my sister Maggie. We are going to California, but that cloud looks bad. Would you allow us to shelter in your shed? There looks as if there might be room for us and our horses."

She stared up at him, her round face crinkling into a network of laugh lines as she smiled. "You go west on Army horse, *sí?* With tiny little pony come along behind. Ver' funny outfit you got. You come in house; shed no good in storm like this one that comes."

Something in her round, solid figure, the good humored lines of her face, and the capable hands, holding the shotgun as if it had grown in them naturally, pleased him. He swung his leg painfully over the cantle of the little saddle and looked down at her.

"Thank you. I'm injured got a slug in my leg, a while back, and we really do need to be indoors."

She chuckled. "Maybe you not think so when you hear noise *estos niños* make! But you come in.

"Teodoro!"

The largest of the four boys stepped forward to lead the horses to one of the sheds, as Magda dismounted and came to Johnny's side.

"Come on, *Caro*. Are you very stiff?" she asked. She lifted her hands and steadied him as he painfully maneuvered his bad leg and looked at the long step to the ground.

"Ah!" said the woman. "You hold this, *niña*. I will lift him down, so!" She reached up and lifted him off the horse as if he were a five-year-old. Steadying him with her shoulder, indeed, half carrying him, she took him into the house and stretched him on one of the bunks lining the walls of the front room.

Magda followed, with three of the boys and the five girls, each carrying some item from the pack horse. The room was cheerful, for a lamp was already lit against the coming darkness, and the cook stove in the corner held simmering pots. The smells rising into the air made Johnny's mouth water as he lay on the bunk, letting his leg rest.

Before Teodoro could return from the shed, the storm came rampaging down from the northwest, flinging handfuls of rain against the stout walls. Shutters closed out most of the weather, although particularly savage gusts cast a fine mist of rain through the cracks where the panels met. The windows, of course, had no glass, though homespun cloth could be pulled across them to shut out some of the draught.

The woman took up the lamp and came to examine her guest. "I am Margarita Consuela Martínes y Wallace," she said, setting down the lamp on a small table.

She bent over him, unselfconsciously pulling down his trousers to get at the wound. "You wonder, I think, how I come to marry a *gringo*? *Mi* Tomás, he is good man, good farmer. Will build big barn, when he get back from this war."

She checked the wound, changed the dressings after swabbing the torn flesh with a dark unguent, and stepped back. "You will do, I think." She pulled a blanket over him. "Once you eat, you will rest."

Johnny, for once lacking the pain that had accompanied him for so many days, lay listening to the women as they talked and worked over the iron cook stove in the corner.

"We are in trouble," Magda told Margarita. "I suspect you guessed that at once. The northerners are probably looking for us; they hanged our parents and shot Johnny. We..."—She stared at the woman for a moment, gave a little nod, and continued—"...killed a whole troop of Yankee cavalry, except for their Captain."

Margarita did not change expression. "Plenty bad thing happen in war," she said. "We must do our best to wash all away, now it is done. You kill Yankees. So have my Tomás kill *many* of them. He had no good cause, as you, for they do not hang his own family. So you go west, eh?"

"It is probably best. Might you let us stay until Johnny is on his feet? We can do a lot to help you around the farm." Magda sounded very young, and Johnny suddenly realized how his wound had made him lean on her. She was only seventeen, however tough and efficient she might try to seem.

Margarita nodded. "I think maybe so. We shall see." And then she dished up a tremendous meal that disappeared magically under the onslaught of nine children and two overstressed acrobats.

The next day, after finding that he could walk with makeshift crutches about the rain-battered farmyard, Johnny got out his knives. As Margarita and her children stared, bewitched, he and Magda juggled, tossed knives, and the girl tumbled and bounced and swung from beams until the watchers looked dizzy.

Then there was no question of letting these newcomers go, as Johnny had suspected might be the case. "We come in tired and dirty from the field, and now we have circus in our own house. Make us laugh, be happy. How could you do any more than that?" asked Margarita, when Magda offered to work in the fields beside the family.

So they rested. The Wallaces, whatever the social shortcomings of their farm, ate well from the bounty of gardens and poultry pens and rabbit hutches, not to mention the small herd of cattle that ranged the north part of the farm. Tomás had left his family well provided for when he went off to war.

After two days of sleeping and eating, Johnny found himself ready to begin getting back into condition. At first he limped about the yard, stretching the scar tissue, making his muscles work again. Then he sat on a long bench and juggled anything the children might fling at him. Sometimes he had kindling wood, pebbles, wood chips from the chopping block, and the random toy or pot all in the air at once.

Within a week, he was beginning the exercises needed to regain his ability to perform as the acrobat he had been reared to be. Magda, though she protested at first, agreed at last to assist him, and the lives of the Wallaces became even more exciting.

Under the scrutiny of his cousin, Johnny began with a cautious program of tumbling. This led, more quickly than Johnny had ever hoped, to more strenuous activities. They rigged parallel bars between two sheds in the cow lot, and Johnny found them adequate as he regained strength and agility.

At first their hostess seemed dubious at such unorthodox treatment for a man so recently wounded. Yet once she saw the furious determination with which Johnny attacked the reconditioning of his body she held her peace.

He worked for weeks, and she was there when he pulled himself into a handstand on the parallel bars.

Though the leg was still stiff, he managed to work around it, going through a series of maneuvers that had the youngsters gasping with excitement. When he finished, he looked down at his audience.

"*Señora*, young masters and mistresses, you have been extremely kind. We have greatly enjoyed our stay among you, but now it is time for us to go. We feel that we are imposing on you, and we also think the Yankees may come here, now that the war is over. That would make trouble for you, if we were found here."

Margarita nodded reluctantly. "I know this time come," she said. "You have been mos' welcome, you and your sister. You have made us joyful, and that is no small thing in these sad days. We have worry about the soldiers, too, however. They hang you, if they catch you. Perhaps they hang us, too. You plan to go tomorrow?"

"Yes," he sighed, dropping onto his feet with hardly a wince.

"We make up big pack of supplies for you. Even the small pony, they will have to help carry things. We will miss you much, *mis niños*, when you go."

* * * * * * *

It was, indeed, a tearful parting. The Wallaces held the same view of tears that the Gannellis did, and floods lubricated their leave-taking. Johnny rode away beside his cousin, the packhorse and the ponies trailing behind, leaving a very damp family in his wake.

It was early, the sun low in the east, casting the shadows of horses and riders long and thin before them toward the west. An omen, he thought.

Yet before noon Magda turned in her saddle (an old one of Thomas Wallace's) to stare back at her cousin. He was already sharing her intuition, his heart thudding with apprehension.

"Something is wrong," he said, before she could speak. "Back there, with those people who were so good to us. Something is badly wrong. We must go back."

She nodded and wheeled her animal to follow him. Johnny nudged his horse into a trot, and followed by the ponies they hurried back eastward toward the Wallace farm.

CHAPTER SEVEN

They hated to pause and rest the horses, though they knew they must. But when they remounted they pushed the animals hard, and in less time than it had taken them to go they came back within sight of the sycamore trees around the house. When those became a smudge at the edge of the horizon, Johnny stopped.

"We mustn't ride in. If something is wrong, our getting caught in the middle will not help Margarita and the children. We must go quietly and carefully, concealed along that line of trees." He pointed toward the windbreak of scrub-oak that Thomas Wallace left along the edge of each plowed field.

They made for the trees, where they tethered the ponies and their packhorse, loosing bits and giving enough slack for them to crop the grass as they waited. Then both Gannellis headed for the house, keeping within the shelter of the hedgerow.

Well short of the cow-lot fence, they dismounted and left their mounts tethered among the last clump of oaks. Johnny reached for one of the Yankee rifles, but at the last minute he felt that handguns and the familiar knives would serve them best.

"Better the weapon you know," he whispered to Magda, as they settled knives into sheaths.

Horses stood in the back yard, some of them stamping among the carefully tended rows of the garden and tearing mouthfuls of greens and bean vines. Because of the thick shrubbery that Margarita had planted around the yard, it was impossible to count the number, but there were several.

As they came nearer, Johnny heard the sound of breaking glass, along with gruff voices of men. As they reached the fence, they could see that at least one was keeping watch on the road that led away to the south.

"Over the top," Johnny whispered to his cousin. She nodded.

Slithering to the corner of the nearest shed, he flowed up its side like a lizard. Magda came after him, and using their abandoned parallel bars they made their way to the roof of the shed nearest the house.

Almost directly before their position a man lounged under one of Margarita's sycamores, his gaze drifting often toward the road, when it was not fixed on the cigarette between his fingers. He was clad in bits of castoff uniforms. His hair was long and full of straw that straggled from beneath the battered hat, whose brim concealed his face. The hand with the cigarette was amazingly dirty.

Johnny was debating with himself whether this man deserved to die, just because he was in a place where he should not be, when there came another crash from the house. It was followed by a shriek and the blast of Margarita's shotgun.

The hand of the guard dropped the cigarette and snaked for his hip. But as he moved, there came a bright flicker through the air, and one of Johnny's knives buried itself in his back. He coughed once and went flat onto his face.

There came a shout, "Hunk! Get in here! This bitch's gone and blowed Henry plumb to bits!"

From the other side of the house came two sets of footsteps, and the front door opened and slammed shut. Johnny leaped down, staggered a bit on landing, and heard

Magda land lightly behind him. She moved toward the back door, silent as a breeze, while Johnny eased around the shrub-obscured wall toward the front.

He stepped, very cautiously, onto the porch and set his ear against the door. Only the sobs of a frightened child came to his ear.

He eased one eye around the window frame opening onto the porch. There was a crack, where the half open shutter stood away from the wall, and through it he saw a man leaning against the door leading into Margarita's bedroom.

Another stood in the middle of the main room, holding Alicia, the oldest girl, by her fine brown hair. She hardly seemed to understand what was happening, for her horrified gaze was fixed on the shattered body on the floor. That must have been the late Henry, Johnny decided.

"This one's too little to be prime stuff," said the man, his wide face cut by a snaggle toothed smile. He gave Alicia a shake. "If they don't leave none of the old lady for us, we'll have to make do with her, I guess."

Augusto, the smallest boy, broke into a howl of terror. "By God, Hunk, knock that kid in the head, will you? He's a pain in the ass," the would-be child rapist said.

The other man moved away from the door of the bedroom and backhanded little Gus against the wall. Johnny heard gasps, as the other children choked back cries of fear. Shaking with fury, he withdrew from the window.

Bending low beneath the level of the partially open shutter, he crossed the porch and moved against the wall of the bedroom. In that room the shutters were closed tightly, but when he put his ear against the wood he heard gasps, choked sobs, and thrashings that told him that dear fat Margarita was receiving the attentions of at least one of the unknown men.

He slid hastily around the house and hissed at Magda until she looked up. "Get onto the roof," he whispered.

"Here, use the shovel. I am going to get at least some of them out of the house. You take care of as many as you can when they come through the door."

He moved toward the tree under which their first victim had stood watch. "Fire!" he roared. "Get out here quick!"

Instantly, he ran to the corner of the house, loosing the knives in their sheaths. Ten heartbeats passed before activity began inside. Feet thundered through the kitchen, and Hunk hove into view, to be met by a terrific *clang* as the shovel met his skull.

The man behind him had no time to react, for Johnny's knife caught him in the throat. But more were on their way, coming in a bunch. "Jim! Hey, Jim! Where's any fire? What's going on?"

Three burst from the doorway together. One went down under Magda's shovel before they reached the scraped dirt of the yard. Johnny's knives were a deadly rain falling onto the other pair before they realized where they were coming from. Johnny drew a deep breath. "You can come down now," he said to Magda, and she skinned the cat onto the ground, landing partially upon the tumble of bodies.

Someone groaned when her boot heels dug into him. The two Gannellis bent over the men and Johnny grabbed the one who had threatened to rape Alicia. He dragged him out of the tangle and whipped him onto his face to tie his hands. But then he stopped and looked more closely.

"Damn! This one's dead, and I would have loved to skin him alive. Slowly."

Again there came a groan, and Hunk showed signs of coming around after having his skull dented with the shovel. Magda lifted the handy implement and whacked him again, after which Johnny tied him securely.

Magda was gazing at the house with dread in her eyes. "Johnny, I think I should see about Margarita. She has been raped, I am certain. That will make a man unwelcome to her eyes, for a time. I must go and see to her."

He nodded, and she went into the house, leaving Johnny to pile the dead into another heap. He tied Hunk securely with clothesline and leaned him against the wall.

When that was done, he went around to the front. "Teodoro!" he called. "I need you, son."

The boy emerged, his face bruised and pale with fury. "They hurt Mama!" he said. "I shall kill them!"

Johnny laid a comforting hand on his shoulder. "They're mostly dead already," he said. "Now I need for you to go down the hedgerow and find all the horses and ponies. One of those bastards is still alive, and I want to keep an eye on him, but I do want the horses right here, hidden in the shed.

"There are probably more of those *figlioli degli diavolo* round about. They usually travel in packs larger than this one would be."

The boy wiped his nose on his sleeve, and with a final sniff he was gone, leaving Johnny to wonder about those others who might possibly be ravaging the farms in the area. These were guerrillas or simply looters. Bad men did run in packs, and a half-dozen wasn't large enough for their kind.

He stepped to the back door and called, "Mag! Margarita! We need to hold a council of war!"

Magda appeared at the door, wiping her eyes. "They hurt her badly, but she is strong. She will be out soon. She is talking with the children now. They were terribly afraid, and a couple were beaten by those...those...I do not know words terrible enough to describe them."

He nodded. "We must get the family away from here into hiding. Did Margarita hear them say anything about others of their group who were not with them?"

Magda's eyes went wide. "I will ask her. What will we do if there are more? These we surprised and dealt with, but others, without that advantage, might be difficult for so few to handle."

"You tell the children to be getting supplies together, while we talk with Margarita and she decides what she wants to do. Teodoro will be here in a bit with the horses, and if she wants to take off for the nearest town she can. There is a wagon in the barn, and all these mounts those scum rode in on will make more than enough riding horses if she doesn't want to take the wagon."

By the time Teodoro returned with the horses, Margarita had pulled herself and her family together. She was a tough woman, with a discipline that had to be seen to be believed.

When she came out of the house she looked Johnny straight in the eyes. "I do not run from *estos diablos*. I keep my house, my stock, my children here for when Tomás return.

"We take all those gun they bring, all the ammunition. They will not find it so easy, if others come looking for this carrion." Her eyes sparked with rage and tears.

Johnny's mind was busy. "You can fort up here, yes. I'll bury those bodies away from the house, and there won't be any way the rest, if there are others, can know they ever came here at all. We'll take enough of their horses to make up the right number and lay a false trail, heading northwest from the road.

Margarita stared at the man against her wall. "He is not dead," she said.

"That can be corrected," said Johnny. "If we take him with us, we may learn something about his bunch. And I also have other plans for him. If we make our trail very... interesting...the rest of them will have no thought for you."

Magda, coming out of the house with a wailing child in her arms, stared at her cousin, her eyes wide. "What do you intend? I do not like the sound of this, Gian-Carlo."

She shushed small Anna against her shoulder. "We are not barbarians, we Gannellis."

Johnny stared down at the unconscious Hunk. "We *were* not, before we came among such people. But there is only one way in which to deal with creatures like that Captain and these *banditti*...we must be more cruel than they."

Margarita took the child from Magda's arms and held it against her massive breast. The girl reached to take Gus's hand and looked about at the rest of the children.

The stood about the adults in a tight clump, their small faces frightened and yet, somehow, determined. "You will post them, like soldiers?" she asked their mother. "Find good spots for them, check their guns...." Her voice was very low and sad. "Poor little ones. It is terrible to have to go to war at such tender ages."

Johnny nodded. "That is the way. Now you go inside, while Teodoro and I bury these animals. And hurry. We have no idea where the others, if others there are, may be, and how soon they will follow their comrades."

CHAPTER EIGHT

Although it seemed that they had been working and fighting and killing for hours, it was only just past noon. Yet now the corpses were buried in the corner of the plowed field that waited for cotton to be planted, and no one would notice more disturbed earth there.

The house had been turned into a fortress, the windows stoutly boarded inside the shutters, with loopholes through which its defenders might shoot, if need be. The doors were reinforced, and it would take a massive attempt to break them down.

The children, as children will, had accepted with flexibility their new duties as guards and defenders. Not one seemed horrified at the thought of shooting men of the kind who had hurt their mother.

Johnny and Magda spent the night, keeping their captive in one of the sheds. Johnny hated having him fed, but Magda overruled him and carried out his food herself. Then she forced her reluctant cousin to take him to the privy to relieve himself.

All the while, Johnny had his hand on a knife, and the nameless bandit made no move to escape. He seemed more terrified of the knives than of any gun.

When they were again ready to move, well before sunrise, Johnny put their prisoner again onto a horse and tied him securely. He had not spoken a word since he revived from his encounter with the shovel, and his eyes tended to wander off in different directions, as if he still suffered from that unexpected impact.

Beneath the grime on his skin, he seemed very pale, and that suited Johnny perfectly. He hoped the wretch was as frightened as the Wallaces had been the day before, and he found himself toying with ideas for making him suffer even more.

This time their leave-taking was even more tearful. Everyone knew that this time there would be little chance that they might meet again, and Johnny found himself sad as he turned westward, once again, and moved away.

Behind, he could hear the thud of the hooves of the other horses. The ponies, as they had the day before, straggled on either side, sometimes galloping ahead and grazing until the procession caught up with them.

They were now traveling across broad country banded with patches of woodland. The land seemed open to the sky, although its contours rolled gently. Grassland was broken frequently by thick files of trees lining the banks of creeks that held, at this time of year, ample water.

They saw no other farm, and that didn't surprise Johnny, for Margarita had told him theirs was the only spread for many miles, and those others lay more to the south and east. It was just as well.

He would have hated to lead anyone who might follow the tracks of the dead raiders' mounts into country inhabited by decent people. The more deserted the countryside, the better it would be for the scheme that was percolating in the head of Gian-Carlo Gannelli.

They kept moving as the sun sank behind a line of trees in the middle distance. They rode in twilight and then in starlight, coming at last into the wooded fringes of a fair-sized stream with high banks.

Wordlessly, the cousins dismounted, hobbled their horses, arranged the packs into an improvised fort, and built a small fire beneath the overhanging bank of the creek, using a small gravel bar as a fireplace.

* * * * * * *

Magda said nothing until the meal was over, though she kept watching her cousin closely. Johnny unloaded the captive and tied him, standing, against a tree trunk in a small glade on the bank above. The man was watching nervously as they went back and forth, taking food from the packs down to the cook fire.

Johnny said nothing to Magda until they had eaten. She noted that he did not offer the man any food, and when she moved to take him something her cousin shook his head with all the authority of his new position of head of the family.

When the meal was done, the pots scoured in the creek, using sand and gravel, and she had begun unrolling her blankets inside the pack fort, Johnny said, "It would be better, Cara, if you take your blankets beyond that thicket. I have some...work...to do. You do not want to see it, I know."

She caught her breath, glancing at the tense shape of the man spread-eagled to the tree. "Oh, Gian-Carlo, I wish you would not...."—but he shook his head fiercely.

"Remember Mama and Papa and Barnabas and Celie? My parents and yours? They were murdered by better men than this. Wishing they would not do it did nothing to stop that terrible thing." He glared at the captive.

"This excuse for a man was going to use Alicia, along with the others, as they did Margarita. A child could not live through such treatment, and far better if she had not, if they had done as they willed." He was pale, now, sweating, even though the spring night was cool.

"If we had not turned back, my little cousin, this would have happened. All those who took us in and tended us and became our friends would have died, and now this one is going to suffer for all those taking part in that terrible thing.

"He should be happy that they were interrupted, for if their plans had been carried out, his death would have been even harder than it will be. I will let him die more quickly. Otherwise, I would have made him last a long, long time."

Without a word, Magda took up her bedroll and moved through the light brush, past the thicket, and out of sight of the tree and of the other fire Johnny had begun kindling in the middle of the small clearing. As she left the spot, she saw the man straining to call out after her, but the dirty gag allowed only a series of grunts to escape.

The white-rimmed eyes rolled after her, as she turned away. She felt a surge of grief that she could not save her cousin from committing this terrible act. She knew that in time to come Johnny would feel the guilt of it as much as his victim would feel the physical pain.

* * * * * * *

Johnny, left with his victim, laughed, and the sound was strange, even to him. "First I think I will show you something of the Gannelli Family Circus. You like the circus? Or have you never seen one?"

He laid the knives on one of the packs, their shining array drawing the gaze of the man irresistibly. "Now you shall see something of my art," Johnny said. He turned his back to the fire, facing the captive.

Then his hands were filled with bright silver flashes, which went whirling madly into the air in an endless curve as he juggled them. Then, without warning, they were whirling toward the shrinking figure against the tree.

"Whick! Whick! Whick! Whick!" The blades bit into the bark, shaving closely against his scalp, his right cheek, his left cheek, and leaving a trickle of blood along the side of his throat.

A groan escaped him. His eyes rolled again, turning up to show the whites, and he slumped in a faint, his whole body seeming to melt against the tree.

Johnny shook his head. This *thing* was supposed to be a wicked man, tough and fearless. What a disappointment! He dipped a bucket of water from the pool beyond the gravel bar and dumped it over his victim.

The eyelids fluttered and opened. The man regarded him with terror-filled eyes.

"You do not like my act? That is a pity, for I was considered very, very good. My grandfather told me that I was worthy to perform before the rulers of Europe, as he and his fathers did. But perhaps you do not appreciate the delicate art of the knives."

He felt a grin crease his cheeks without any warmth at all. "I think that you will like something you understand more fully. I have heard that the Indians do wonderful things with fire and a blade. Perhaps I should perfect my skills in that area."

He bent over the fire, and there came a moan from the bound figure. When he straightened, he began removing the ragged uniform from the prisoner, leaving his torso bare in the firelight. He noticed with amusement that his captive had his eyes tightly closed, as if what he could not see would not harm him.

"This will not do at all!" he protested. "One must see this to appreciate it. But I have been told of a useful technique the Indians use. That is just what I shall do."

The gag muffled terrible sounds from the man as Johnny worked about his eyes with one of the scalpel-sharp knives. When he stepped back, the eyeballs stared, lidless, from the bloody sockets.

"Now you will have to watch what I do. I no longer believe, as Mama taught me, that there is a useful devil in

Hell to work retribution upon your kind. I must take the task upon myself.

"What you helped to do to Margarita and her family was certainly not your first sin against humanity. So I shall take into consideration all those others that you have done, alone and in company with those *banditti* we killed. Everything will be paid for at once.

"That is only just, do you not agree?"

* * * * * * *

Magda, who had thought herself out of earshot, heard every word. She wept soundlessly, muffling her sobs with her blanket, suffering every step of that long night with Johnny's victim.

She moved farther away, out of range of the sounds, but there was no rest, however she turned and wriggled. Rearranging her bedroll did not help. Even though she could not hear the sounds now, they echoed in her mind, each one piercing her heart.

Had it been Johnny's wound and the subsequent fever that had done this? Had the deaths of their parents turned his mind? Had the weeks of inactivity, while his wound healed, driven her gentle cousin Gian-Carlo quite mad?

CHAPTER NINE

Magda woke when dawn lit the sky beyond the tree-tops above her. She folded her blankets and crept through the brush and deadfall to the clearing, where she found Johnny deeply asleep, his face strange and forbidding, with its dark stubble of beard and the new, cruel lines about the mouth.

She found herself afraid to wake this strange, fearful cousin. Instead, she moved quietly to the tree where the body of the prisoner hung, now obviously dead. Those staring, lidless eyes were no longer filled with suffering. Death, she imagined, had come as a friend, after such a night.

She gulped down bile and turned to gather twigs and leaves for starting a fire among the embers of Johnny's blaze of the night before. Blowing on the flickers of flame distracted her mind from the terrible object on the tree.

The sun had not risen, although the sky was growing bright. The horses had moved close, cropping the grass under the trees, and both ponies nuzzled close to her when she stood up after getting the fire going well. She fondled them, murmuring to them the Italian love words they knew.

She felt guilty. It had been a long time since she had the time to reassure the little creatures, and they had obviously missed being treated as the pets they had always been.

Something about the tension of the night before, the freshness of the morning, the need to leave behind the torn body on the tree made her leap onto the back of Pietro, the white pony. "Hup!" she commanded, returning for the moment to her childhood of training.

The small beast tucked in its chin and began moving: she rode him down into the creek's wide bend, where the water was shallow and the gravel footing was firm. Trotting in a circle, the pony took up the steady rhythm it had been taught, and Magda rose to her knees, at last balancing on one foot, as her mother had taught her when she was two years old.

She extended her arms and raised her free leg behind her in an arabesque, higher and higher, her arms curved like wings. As the pony came around, she saw that Johnny stood on the bank above, the strained look gone, for the moment, from his face.

He whistled, and the black pony leaped down into the creek bed, taking up the pace of its companion. Johnny flipped off the bank, landing on both feet, his knees flexing with the stride of the animal. He went into a handstand on the broad shoulders of the beast, and for a moment Magda felt that the past weeks must be a weird nightmare. This was their normal life.

She could almost hear the rhythmic sounds of Mama's accordion and Papa's plaintive violin, playing the *March of the Comedians* or the *Poet and Peasant Overture*. Pulling the ponies side by side with whistled signals, the two changed mounts, leaping smoothly from back to back.

Now Magda stood on her hands and Johnny balanced on one foot, laughing like children as the ponies paced. The sun was up, and the stream chattered cheerfully below. Playing so, the girl found her heart growing lighter than it had been in a long while.

Then her cousin sprang down from Pietro's back and signaled to the black to stop. "We must go," he said. "The rest of those bushwhackers may come at any time, following what they think may be their companions. I must have time to leave a message for them."

Magda found her light mood popped like a bubble. She turned toward him, feeling anguish in her heart. "I would have thought the message you tied to that tree would be enough for anyone."

"That is only a part of it. There must be no chance of any mistake. I want them to understand that they are pursuing a deadly enemy. I want them to have no time to think of anything else...not of backtracking and perhaps finding Margarita and her children.

"I will write a note and pin it to that man on the tree. It will surely bring them after us."

"And then what?" she asked, her throat tight with fear.

He looked puzzled. Magda leaned forward and set her hand on his arm. "Then what, Gian-Carlo? When they follow us and there are, after all, only two of us what happens then? We have many skills, but we are not trained to fight. Not with guns and fists.

"We are not soldiers, not even so much as scum like those. Do you think we will be able to kill them all? There may be a dozen more, you said. And when they have killed you, what do you think will happen to me? I am not large enough to fight them all off." Her tone grew fierce. "I will endure what Margarita endured, and no one will come to rescue me!" She stared up into his eyes, willing her cousin to return to his senses.

Johnny turned pale, the ruff of black curls over his brow seeming even darker by contrast. His eyes, which had seemed to be focused on something inside him, shifted their expression to one of dawning horror.

"Cara! What have I done? I did not think of you—you have always seemed like my second self or my right hand. I had not considered what being a woman might mean to you." He sounded choked.

"Forgive me, little cousin! I have been obsessed, I think. Perhaps I have been a bit mad."

She began to smile, but that froze on her face as she glanced past his shoulder toward the bank from which he had sprung onto the pony. In turn, she felt herself turning pale.

Johnny, his gaze on her face, went still. Then he pivoted slowly and looked up at an Indian who watched them both from the bluff.

The man was not alone. Several dark shapes bulked against the morning sky, two mounted and bearing shields decorated with feathers. Four stood now beside the first, but that was the one to whom her gaze returned. He was obviously the leader, by inches, by bearing, and by innate nature. She had never seen a more commanding person in all her life.

A crunching of hooves in leaves came to her ears, and a whinny told her that the horses they had brought were being rounded up. A youth sprang into the creek bed and drove the ponies to his waiting fellows. Then the tall leader spoke in a guttural tongue to the young man and pointed toward the cousins.

* * * * * * *

Johnny stared up into the enigmatic face of the savage. Then he reached for Magda's hand and led her up to the top of the bluff, where they found their own horses waiting in a bunch. The packs left in the clearing had been opened and two of the Indians moved forward to join the ones rummaging through the supplies.

The shock of this sudden disaster had brought him back to his wits, after a long time of withdrawn anguish that bordered on insanity. He thanked what fortune was left to him that his knives were concealed about his person in their hidden sheaths. Unless he was stripped, no one would suspect their existence.

His thought was interrupted by the tall Indian, who motioned for him to follow and moved toward the dead man spread-eagled against the tree. Once there, the leader surveyed the corpse critically, examining Johnny's handiwork with every evidence of admiration.

Then he turned with a strangely French gesture, as if to inquire if Johnny had been the one who did this. Johnny nodded, pointing to the dead man, then to himself.

"Yes. He was my enemy, and I killed him." His voice sounded strange, even to himself.

That inscrutable face did not change as the Indian looked again at the corpse, again at him, and shrugged. "Extremely effective work for a white man," he said, in an accent so cultured that Johnny was dumbfounded.

What sort of man was this Indian into whose hands they had fallen?

CHAPTER TEN

Johnny heard Magda gasp. He felt disoriented, as if the solid ground were crumbling beneath his feet. "Who are you?" he managed to ask, keeping his voice level. "You don't...look as if you might speak English."

That dark face, striped with intricate white lines, smiled. It made an astonishing difference in his expression. Instead of an anonymous painted savage, the Indian became an individual person a rather likeable one, Johnny found to his surprise.

"My people call me Potesenaquahip," he said, rolling the impossible name off effortlessly. "That is an excellent name for one of my kind, for it means Buffalo Hump. After your sort drove us from our hunting lands, we found starvation to be a problem. Many of us are named for food." His smile broadened, as if he appreciated their bafflement at his command of their tongue.

"I was captured by Cheyenne on a journey across the plains. They sold me to a Frenchman, who traded me to an Englishman traveling through the West. He took me back to his own country, when he went, and there he had me schooled by one of his secretaries. I can read Latin, if you can believe such a thing of a barbarian."

Looking into those highly intelligent eyes, Johnny had no doubt of the truth of his statement. This was no wild Indian, that was certain.

"But he returned to this country on a diplomatic mission, and I took the opportunity to escape. Knowing at first hand the ways of the white men, I chose to find my own kind again and live a life unhampered by alien traditions, uncomfortable clothing, and ridiculous assumptions.

"But my own tribe is gone, dead or incorporated into the remnants of others. I found others of the Comanche, and now I am a sort of War Chief, though that does not conform to any idea you may have of command or authority.

"We have done our bit, while the locals have been away fighting their own war. And it seems that you..."—he glanced aside at the tattered body—"...have a war of your own in progress, as well."

Johnny knew that he should have been terrified, both for himself and for his cousin. But suddenly he felt easy, confident that this was someone he could trust. "I am happy to meet you, Pota-what?"

"Call me Senaqua," said the Indian. "That is easier for a white tongue. It is what the Englishman called me."

Johnny nodded. "Well, Senaqua, I was beginning to worry that I had put my cousin into a bad situation. We're being followed, I am almost certain, by a bunch of bushwhackers like this one. Bad men, believe me. But you seem to be a civilized man, and maybe she will not be in as much danger as I feared."

The engaging smile disappeared as if it had never existed. Senaqua again looked completely barbaric. "I am not what you might call civilized. I was introduced to that curious way of life, embraced it with as much pretended enthusiasm as was required to regain my freedom, but I was never convinced that it was a rational way of living.

"No, when I took off the drawers and collars and other appurtenances of civilized usage, I fear that I also removed any trace or taint that they might have left upon my character. I have rejected civilization, if you take my meaning."

He turned to stare at his fellows, who were dressing themselves in shirts and Magda's petticoats that she had brought in case she might need them. He half smiled.

"What do you call yourselves?" he asked, in that drawing room accent that fitted so badly with his appearance.

Gannelli sighed. "I am Gian-Carlo Gannelli. I am now calling myself, for several reasons, Johnny Gann. This is my cousin Magda.

"Some weeks ago, we watched a troop of Yankees hang our parents. We managed to survive, and then we went back and killed most of that troop. We ran south and west across the river into Texas, and it is not only bushwhackers who may follow us. In time, I suspect that the victors in this late war will be after us, too."

Senaqua stared away into the grasslands, as if thinking hard. "The youth is a woman? I took her for a boy. Where did the two of you learn to ride in such a weird manner?"

Johnny felt a sudden weight of weariness fall upon him, and he gestured toward a blanket that had been flung down nearby. "Could we sit down? I was badly wounded when they attacked us, and this is a long story."

Senaqua nodded and sank, straight-backed, onto the blanket. The two joined him, and Johnny said, "Your Englishman must never have taken you to the circus."

"No, he did not. What is a circus?" Johnny began the long tale of the family's wanderings and ended it with his night of entertaining the dead man. When he was done, the Indian looked at him with some respect.

"So you have fought for your own kind, as I have. And your cousin is a warrior, too? We have such women among our kind, though not often. We Comanche are all fierce and proud, and we do not let offenses against our people go unpunished."

He was silent a moment, and Johnny thought he saw the merest crinkle of a smile touch the painted cheek nearest him. "So you are at war with the entire nation, eh?"

He said no more, and they sat watching the others in the party pilfering through the packs like a troop of monkeys. Senaqua seemed not to see them, but instead was evidently thinking hard. At last he glanced up at Johnny and nodded. Then he rose, as effortlessly as a deer.

Johnny and Magda got to their feet, as well. As Johnny stared into the black eyes of the Comanche, he saw what seemed a twinkle in the depths beneath the prominent brows.

"Perhaps the civilized ways went deeper than I knew," said Senaqua. "I find myself tempted to change our traditions. Muguara or Esanap would take a day or so to conduct you into death, and then they would take your woman and give her to one of the tribe as wife. That would be that.

"Yet I find myself intrigued by the fact that the two of you managed to wipe out a troop of cavalry, even though you were wounded. We have had encounters with those troops, and they are not easy to eliminate. It fills me with admiration."

He sighed heavily. "My men are of the old school, however. It is hard to turn them from the traditional methods, no matter what argument I may present. I would love to make an impressive show of your prowess, in order to demonstrate your value. Do you think you might manage such a thing?"

Johnny glanced down at Magda and swallowed hard. There had been times, often, when the survival of his group had depended upon the quality of the performances they could wring from their hungry bodies. But never had death by torture been the penalty for failure.

He was weary, not entirely conditioned after his wound. Much would depend upon Magda's strength and courage. And the thought of either of them spending such a night as he had given his captive filled him with cold horror.

"I think, if we have a moment to talk and to plan, we may be able to persuade your people of our usefulness," Johnny said at last.

Magda, of course, was already making plans. "There are two trees beyond the thicket, where I spent the night," she told him. "They have smooth branches that are almost parallel to the ground. They are high enough to allow maneuvering room.

"We might do acrobatics and fixed-bar routines. Then the knives; all of mine are in place, all unsuspected, as yet. As are yours."

He nodded, and slowly he began to grin. "You are a brick, Cara. Who but a Gannelli, faced with hardship, decision making, and the possibility of torture, could think so clearly. Come, let us begin."

They found that a number of branches had to be trimmed in order to allow their passage above those chosen as their bars. When that was done, they returned to the clearing, for it was best for the first part of their planned entertainment. There was room enough there for the ponies to trot in a small circle.

As they worked to prepare their ground, the pair talked softly, outlining the routines they would use. So ingrained were the movements of all their repertoire that altering the order was nothing to either.

When they were done, the sun was high. The horses were being held in the hollow below the creek bank, and they stood flicking their tails at flies, half dozing, with their heels cocked lazily.

When Johnny whistled, clicking his fingers, the ponies woke and scampered up the slope into the improvised ring. But they snorted and shied until the corpse was removed, for the smell of his death disturbed the small beasts.

Then they steadied and began their metronome-like pace around the circle that Johnny had marked on the scuffed dirt. The first act of the Comanche Special Performance of Circus Gannelli was about to begin.

CHAPTER ELEVEN

Gian-Carlo Gannelli peeled to his underdrawers, in lieu of purple tights and tunic. Magda took off her floppy shirt and pulled on a sweater that was tight enough not to impede her motions. Then, hearing in their minds the cadences of violin and accordion, they held hands, bowed, and stepped into the ring.

Senaqua had persuaded his group to leave the game they had begun playing. That involved a buffalo robe that had been crosshatched with white lines, onto which they flipped short sticks by tapping their ends on a stone just as they released them.

Leaving the sticks exactly as the last turn had placed them, the Indians moved to take their places at one side of the clearing. They sat patiently, waiting, seeming to have all the time in the world to waste. They seemed to be without the driving impatience of white men, their minds turned toward some unguessable internal landscape which was invisible to one of Johnny's color.

Senaqua was impassive now, seemingly all Indian. His smile might never have been, as he called a guttural comment to his fellows.

There was a tightness in Johnny's chest even worse than the one he had felt when he was three and took his place, for the first time, in the ring. He had gone aloft with Mama, made simple swings into Papa's strong hands, and returned to the platform beside his mother. The sea of faces, the spatter of applause, had made the moment great and terrible.

This was going to be much more frightening. Clumsiness at this point might sentence them both to a terrible fate. He glanced aside at his cousin, and that knowledge was in her eyes. However, she stepped forward firmly beside him and turned to face the ponies.

"Hup!" cried Magda. The little creatures twitched their ears without altering their steady pace around the circle. Johnny leaped, flipped in midair, and landed securely on the white pony, his feet finding the familiar humps and hollows of its back.

In her turn, Magda ran, made two handsprings, and landed back-to-back with him on Pietro. The two flexed easily with the motions of the pony as it made a complete circuit of the ring.

Johnny whistled piercingly. The black drew alongside his fellow, and Magda made a bridge of her body, setting her hands onto the black's back. Then she was in a handstand on the other pony.

Johnny bent double, settled his palms firmly on the shoulders of the white, and arrowed his feet into the air. Side by side they circled before exchanging mounts, still supported by their hands and arms.

The Indians said nothing, but their eyes had grown very bright and watchful. Johnny risked a side glance at Senaqua as he rounded the ring and found a twitch of amusement curling one side of the thin lips.

They came to their feet again, one on each mount, and clasped their hands. With an effortless spring, Magda was standing on Johnny's shoulders. Again they went around before she vaulted to the ground, rolling to her feet. Johnny followed her at once.

The rhythm of the performance had taken hold of them both. Even lacking actual music, they heard it in their minds, for the cadences were drilled into their bones.

Magda spun to the right, Johnny to the left. The girl set her back to a tree—not the one to which the bandit had been tied—raising her hands above her head. Knives blurred from Johnny's hands, outlining her slight body with a stiff fence of steel, set into the gray-brown bark.

There was the faintest of stirs among the Indians. They knew knife work, if little else of this alien craft. They had never, Johnny suspected, seen anything at all like this.

Gannelli backed against a tree and spread his hands, fingers stiffly apart, against the trunk. Magda spun a bright bridge of steel between them, putting a knife into each space between his fingers.

Now there was time to watch Senaqua, for Johnny never worried about his cousin's accuracy. While she worked, the chief was almost smiling, though his mouth was nearly straight. The deep lines from nose to chin had relaxed their severity.

Johnny stepped away, turned, and spun the blades back to his cousin, who picked them from the air as if they had been butterflies. She sent them whirling back, and they juggled knives in concentrated silence, now, never missing a catch or a return, creating the rhythm that kept them from being cut.

He nodded to her, as she caught, flung, caught, flung the blades as she took hers from the air, setting them into a tight circle in the tree trunk.

She returned his own to him, and he turned to flip them into a smaller circle inside the one she had formed. The blades hissed and rang against each other as they zipped into place.

In silence, Johnny took her hand and turned to face their audience. They bowed deeply.

This time there was a difference in the set of those stony features. It was detectable even through the paint, and the youth who had gone after the ponies was hard put to keep his boyish features suitably enigmatic. A glint of pure delight was plain in his dark eyes.

Johnny raised his hands, although the Indians did not applaud, and said, "If you will now follow us, we will show you a tremendous display of aerial daring and skill."

The Comanche rose and came after the pair as they made their way through the brambly thicket to the prepared trees. The horizontal branches extended over the thicket on one side, but on the other they thrust out over the creek bed.

Johnny caught Magda's hands. Lifting her into a handstand, he flipped her into the tree. She caught a branch, drew herself up in an effortless motion, and began rolling over and over the branch.

Johnny's palms ached in sympathy, for he knew the raw bark must be abrading her skin badly. But he caught a branch above his head, swung his feet higher than his head, and found his own level, where he performed every feat of strength, agility, and balance that he could call to mind. He was getting very tired before he stopped. His strength had not returned fully, even with Margarita's coddling and good food, but he knew that he must show no sign of weakness. He continued until he felt that one more swing, one more handstand, one more motion would leave him unconscious below the tree.

Then he whistled sharply, heard Magda grunt in reply, and swung out into a somersault that ended in a firm landing on the ground below the tree. As he glanced about at the Comanche, he saw expressions of veiled approval on several of the faces.

Senaqua was smiling openly, and Johnny drew a deep breath, quelling the trembling of his legs. Magda grimaced wearily, her lips forming the words, "I think they approve."

There came a long time of talk among their captors. Gutturals rumbled like thunder around the circle of warriors, now seated again about their neglected game. Pote-senaquahip sat impassively, listening and occasionally inserting a word, though he seemed indifferent to the outcome of the debate.

Not even by the flicker of an eyelash did he acknowledge the existence of the two whites, sitting at a distance on a blanket. He seemed to have no concern about the decision.

Johnny sat with his cousin beneath one of the trees, watching the sky turn orange with sunset. Clouds were coming in from the north, but the sun slanted from the west, striking through beneath the cloud layer to touch the tops of the trees with rose color.

As he gazed over the grasslands toward the distant and invisible Wallace farm, Johnny found himself remembering his other pursuers. He turned to Magda. "I wonder about Margarita and the children. If there were other bushwhackers, did they find the farm? And will they come after us? They might be right over the edge of the horizon right now!"

A furrow appeared between her fine brows. "True. Should we speak to Senaqua about them? Of the two groups, I believe that I prefer the Comanche."

Staring at her in shock, Johnny found to his amazement that he agreed. He must warn their present captors that they might soon find themselves with unwanted visitors.

CHAPTER TWELVE

Johnny found himself staring covertly at the muttering circle of Comanche. What was the proper way in which to interrupt a powwow, given urgent need?

"Do you think they'll scalp me?" he asked Magda.

"No." She grinned, her face pale now that the flush of exercise had faded. "You were born to be hanged, as they used to say in Arkansas. Remember? That is a good guarantee that you will never be scalped."

"Thank you, Cara. That helps my feelings a great deal," he said in a sarcastic tone. He rose stiffly to his feet, feeling the long ache of the scar down his thigh.

When he turned toward the Comanche, he found Senaqua's gaze upon him, although the Indian's head had not turned. Johnny raised his hand and beckoned, wishing that he knew sign language. Surely this would tell the war chief that he needed to speak with him!

The tall Indian rose from the circle and turned to his captives, leaving the rest to argue the case away without interruption. "You have something to say?" the Comanche asked.

Johnny stepped close. "I told you that we might be followed, I think, when we first met. Now I feel the need to warn you that time enough has passed for anyone who might be following my cousin and me to arrive here on our trail."

"Indeed," came the cool reply.

"I may not have made it clear enough. Those who follow, if they come, will have good reason to come fast, for we have had one of their band. That one against the tree. They will probably be angry, too.

"By nightfall they could arrive, if they picked up the trail of those familiar horse tracks fairly quickly." He searched the white striped countenance for any sign of interest.

"You know, I am certain, about guerrillas, the outriders to the war who have scavenged the countryside. These will be of that kind."

The black eyes did not change their expression, but an indefinable tautness enveloped the skin-clad figure. "Oh? Of that sort, are they?" Senaqua stared off across the grasslands, now dim with twilight.

"We have had our own encounters with that kind. They are not particular whose homes they rob, whose women they rape, or whose children they kill."

Johnny sighed with relief. "We thought you ought to know who will probably come rampaging over the rise tonight. We have decided that we prefer your company, whatever that entails, over theirs. Ten to one."

There came a deep chuckle from the Comanche. The last glow from the west struck through a gap in the thicket to turn him into a coppery statue, standing quite still. Then he grunted and turned to interrupt his companions.

He spoke rapidly and decisively. Gutturals rolled from his tongue, rousing his listeners to something approaching animation. When he paused, the warriors sat for a moment, motionless and thoughtful. Then an affirmative syllable dropped into the fading day, and the entire group rose.

Senaqua looked back at the two whites. The last ray, full on his face, revealed to Johnny the slow wink, invisible to those on his other side. Then he was surrounded by his fellows, and more talk ensued, with frequent glances in their direction assuring Johnny that he and his cousin must figure prominently in the discussion.

The sun went down. The trees shut away the last of the light lingering in the sky, and the young Comanche horse handler began gathering deadfall, arranging it carefully.

Senaqua stopped him and kicked apart his careful circle of sticks. Johnny realized that the Comanche wanted a white man's fire built, rather than the sort the Indians used. The youth began again, setting the wood in the more haphazard pattern used by whites.

After watching for a time, he turned to Magda. "Senaqua, wise old bird that he is, knows anyone coming would recognize an Indian fire, so he wants one that isn't suspicious. I wonder what he's planning."

Once the war chief finished watching the fire-building, he sent the other Comanche to hide among the trees and bushes, where they disappeared with the facility of a bunch of squirrels.

Then he approached the Gannellis. "If they come, they will find a camp with one woman in sight. Your cousin. That should prove irresistible, though they will know that you must be somewhere nearby. They will feel themselves more than a match for a single man.

"We are now arranging that they become even more enraged, for my companions are returning the body you entertained last night to a tree at the southern end of this grove.

"If they come, he will be the first thing they see by the light of the quarter moon. And then they will see this firelight flickering in the distance." He watched Johnny, his eyes dark pits in his aquiline face.

Johnny felt a surge of excitement. "I told you he was a wily old bird. That is what I would do, in his shoes." He turned from Magda to Senaqua, who now, in the fading light, was more a shadow than a man.

"What then?" he asked him.

The Comanche said nothing for a moment; then he sighed. "I have been, you must remember, spoiled by my contact with your kind. Things that delight my peers leave me sad and sick. Although I will not object aloud to what they will do to those following you, if our plan is successful, I dislike what they plan for you.

"Your skills are so unfamiliar to them that they have no measure by which to value them. Your antics amused them, but they still see you only as a captive to be tortured to death and your cousin as a female, who has other pleasant uses. I am sure you understand me.

"There will be much confusion, if those others come. Prisoners are often known to escape at such times. Your horses may be unguarded, for Mugual becomes excited and often leaves his post to take part in a fight."

Johnny felt a great sense of relief. He had wondered about this man, and now he knew. He would hate to betray his own, but he intended to do just that.

Magda reached for his hand in the darkness and squeezed to show that she, too, understood the offer that had been made.

Senaqua said, "The young woman must put on a skirt, if she possesses one. She must tend the fire, stir a pot over the coals. But first we will eat, for there is not yet any sign of anyone approaching."

The fire remained unkindled, and they ate jerky from parflèche bags, and Johnny and Magda finished the cold cornpone Margarita had sent with them. Then Mugual, the youngest Comanche, struck a blaze, using white man's flint and steel. He puffed and blew until a thread of smoke and a glow of red showed among the heaped wood.

Magda dug into the mess of clothing the Comanche had stuffed back into the packs, searching for her only skirt. When she had it about her, she pushed the packs back into the bushes out of sight. Then Senaqua gestured for her to take her place beside the fire, where the Indians had arranged a blanket and a pot, into which they put water and enough jerky to smell like cooking.

Johnny melted into the bushes with the war chief beside him. The Indians had placed their horses up-creek with those of the Gannellis. They equipped them with the saddles to save keeping up with the tack and put Mugual in charge.

The darkness smelled of mud, wet gravel, water, cottonwoods, Indians, and horse droppings. Johnny could hear nothing. If the Comanche had set up a system of watches, he had no way of knowing what the signal might be, for he heard no sound of movement.

Nobody breathed heavily as if sleeping. The night grew blacker outside the ring of firelight. Clouds moved up even more thickly, covering the faint sprinkling of stars and the quarter moon.

Johnny crouched against a tree trunk, dozing now and again, though when his head dropped forward he woke quickly. He had taken little rest the night before, and the day had been very hard. The lack of sleep was telling on him now.

Time dragged on. Magda added wood to the blaze, stirred her pot, which now smelled genuinely like food cooking, and the crickets made a din along the creek bank. A deep-voiced frog woke Johnny at last to full alertness.

Though there was no sound from the Indians, the atmosphere had changed. Expectation filled the air, and now, his eyes grown used to the dark, he could see Senaqua leaning forward, tense beside him. Far off there was the sound of hooves thumping tiredly into hard soil.

Johnny found his breath coming short. To be unarmed, facing those men, seemed unbearable. Then something touched his side. The bag containing his and Magda's knives slid beneath his elbow, and he clamped it tightly against his side to keep it from jingling. A hand touched his shoulder lightly, tapping once, twice, three times, deliberately, and withdrew. Senaqua was sending him a message, and in it he found hope.

In the distance, he heard the snort of a horse. Johnny closed his eyes, straining to interpret those enigmatic taps. Senaqua, it was evident, wanted the Gannellis to escape. He had already told them where the horses were held, and he had returned their knives. The weapons were in the bushes nearby.

Rifles and handguns: those were the things without which it would be folly to try crossing this troubled countryside. Those were piled haphazardly out of sight at the side of the camp, and he strained to recall just where, with relation to his present position, they were. And then he remembered what his conscience had tried to make him forget.

Mugual had bundled them away behind the trunk of the tree to which his captive had been tied. Johnny turned his head, almost able to see the glint of black eyes, though Senaqua's head was a dim oval against the darkness of the trees.

He reached to touch the Indian's buckskin sleeve, three light taps. A single soft exhalation told him that Potesenaquahip understood his signal.

Now the sounds of approaching horsemen were unmistakable, for the night was very still and without any breeze. Magda, in the clearing beside the fire, moved out of her blanket and began poking up the fire around the pot, which was emitting the fragrance of boiling meat.

"Who's there?" she called. There was no fear in her voice, and Johnny felt great pride in her staunchness. She was no vaporish lady, his little cousin.

"We've got 'em," a rough voice rasped. The crackle of brush under hooves told the watchers that the newcomers were riding into the strip of woodland. Then, "Just a woman, dammit!"

"Don't be a bigger fool than your mother made you," said another voice. "No woman's going to be out here all by herself. There's a man here someplace. Sim, you cut around toward the north and see if you can locate him. We'll find out pretty quick if we can get anything out of Miss Pretty here."

A sorrel moved into the firelight. A burly man in a filthy poncho swung down to confront Magda, who stood, arms folded, watching him. He moved near, stared up and down her slender shape, and knocked her flat.

Johnny tensed, but Senaqua's touch held him in place.

"Now that's just a little love tap to let you understand who's the boss here." The big fellow grinned, which was almost worse than his frown would have been.

"We've come a long way, following our own horses' tracks. We're tired to death, and we're mad, because we just found poor Hunk tied to a tree, down yonder a ways, looking as if Injuns had been at him."

He pushed his bearded face close to hers. "Somebody bushwhacked our boys at a farm back there. We sent 'em to check it out and they never got back, which tells us they're dead or hurt so bad they can't ride or walk. We tried to get close enough to find out, but I never seen such a storm of lead in all my life. Couldn't get close enough to tell.

"But we found those tracks, leading north and west, and we've been following ever since. You're going to tell us what we want to know, or you'll wish you had."

Magda looked into his eyes, and her voice was perfectly calm. "Why should I tell you? I know that you will kill me, eventually, whatever I do. Why should I give you any satisfaction at all?"

"There's ways to die, and then there's other ways to die," said the raider. He reached toward his patient horse and took a leather strap from behind the saddle. "Some is worse than others, by a long shot. Now tell me...where's your man?"

"I have no man," she said. "I travel with my cousin, who is the only family I have."

"Then, dammit, where's your cousin?" He raised the strap for a blow.

"He went back into those trees a while ago. I would not advise you to follow him. He had no trouble dealing with your henchmen, back there at the farm. He was the one who entertained your man Hunk last night." She managed a laugh. "You certainly don't want to meet him, whether you know it or not."

He swung his fist and knocked her flat again. She came up effortlessly, her life of falls as an acrobat having left her used to bruises and aches. Now she resumed her upright stance, arms crossed, eyes fixed scornfully on her questioner.

He turned to shout into the dark trees, "Hey, Sim! See anything? There's a man back in there someplace. Hiding behind his woman's skirts!"

There came no reply, Sim being entirely too dead to answer his leader. That silence seemed to trouble the big man. Seven more of the bandits had ridden into the clearing and dismounted, and now they stared about the dark circle of trees beyond the firelight.

"It took some tough *hombre* to take out the boys, back yonder," one of them ventured. "You think we've rid into some kind of ambush?"

The leader turned, his grizzled beard bristling. "They wasn't that many horses. Just three was rode, besides our critters, and two more was little bitty things. Colts, most likely. Nothing but midgets could of rode 'em."

He gestured toward the trees again. "Neddy, you take two of the boys and check to see where Sim is. He must've went down into the creek so he couldn't hear when I yelled."

The three men started toward the trees but stopped in their tracks almost at once. They seemed, there in the ruddy firelight, to have turned to stone.

"Dammit, I said go look for Sim! Can't none of you do nothing without I show you how?"

Before his words were well past his lips, the three fell slowly forward, arrow shafts bristling from their backs. The big man lunged toward the fire and kicked it into flying chunks and sparks. In the sudden darkness there was the sound of men scrambling for cover.

Johnny broke from Senaqua's side and wriggled around the edge of the clearing toward the spot he had imprinted on his brain. Magda was there, and the guns were behind the big oak. He devoutly hoped she had hit the dirt, for he heard arrows whicking through the darkness, their music interrupted by an occasional gunshot.

Circling cautiously, he came at last to the tree on which the unlucky Hunk had died. His foot touched something, and he felt about with both hands, finding the three rifles, the four gun belts with the revolvers in their holsters. He bundled them into his arms and hissed sharply into the blackness.

There came a movement beyond the tree. "Gian-Carlo?"

He sighed with relief. "*Cara*, come quietly."

Quiet as an Indian herself, she moved around the tree to join him, and he felt her hand brush past his chest and return to find his elbow. Silently, she took one of the rifles and a couple of the gun belts, relieving him of the awkward load.

Johnny oriented himself in the darkness. Allowing for his trek around the clearing, Mugual had to be off to their right, in the smaller clearing where Senaqua told him the horses were being held.

The battle was growing in intensity, though he wondered how the bandits could find anything at which to shoot. But they seemed to be filling the dark wood with lead, and he and Magda crept along the leafy space beneath the worst tangle formed by the branches of the brush.

The Indians had rifles, Johnny knew. Now they were using them, their deeper notes very distinct and different from the lighter pops of the handguns. With such an uproar behind them, it was easy for Johnny to keep his bearings.

They moved deeper into the tangle, and the din was somewhat muffled by the heavy growth. Then, ahead, Johnny heard the thump of a hoof and a whicker. He turned to whisper one word into Magda's ear. "Packs."

She knew where they had been put, for their Comanche benefactor had managed to convey that as well. She moved from his side softly, and he knew she would find them if she had to feel out the entire circle around the grassy space.

He eased forward, wondering if Mugual would recognize any sound that was different from the noise of the battle behind them. At the edge of the small space, he lay flat and looked upward, silhouetting anything out in the open against the slightly paler sky. Anyone on watch might be standing, listening to the gunfire.

He saw the bulks of horses, but there was no sign of Mugual. He suspected that the youngster had gone to join his fellows, unable to keep away from a real battle.

Deciding to risk all, he rose and grunted in his gruffest voice, trying to sound like Senaqua. "Mugual!"

Only the whifflings of the horses came in reply. Johnny slipped into the open and caught them, feeling for the bridles that would identify those he and Magda had brought. The bits had been eased, and he slipped them back into their mouths. Then he whistled for the ponies, and at once he heard the sound of little hooves moving on soil.

Magda reappeared, dragging two fat packs. "The saddles are over there. Lead the animals over, and I'll help saddle them." She sounded more excited than frightened.

In ten minutes they were loping away into the grassland, heading due north without crossing the stream. The sky was dark, the west marked with high wisps of cloud that held a trace of light, the east covered with thick batts of darkness broken by slender strips of stars.

Johnny got his bearings and turned toward the west. It seemed that the participants in the battle would be in no condition to pursue them, whoever won, but he intended to take no chances. They had headed north in the beginning. It might just delay any pursuit a bit if they swung due west. And then again, it might not.

CHAPTER THIRTEEN

They crossed the creek, which flowed roughly north-west-to-southeast, and found themselves in flattish country broken by thick stands of scrubby oak. The sky, clearing as the night went on, brightened with stars, and they found it relatively easy to make some speed across the rolling land. After their long rest, the horses were fresh, and they managed to cover many miles before dawn lit the eastern horizon.

While the horses had been rested, their riders were not. Tension and muscle-cracking effort and emotional stress had laid their burdens upon both the cousins, and when another long strip of trees loomed against the west, marking still another creek, both welcomed the sight.

Magda reached between the horses to tap her cousin. "Can we stop and camp? My rear is rubbed raw, and my knees are about to come apart."

He turned his mount's head toward a thick patch of timber. "I thought you'd never ask," he moaned, as they pulled up and dismounted.

They settled the horses for a night of grazing, and turned their attention toward making camp. "We must risk a fire," Johnny said. A rumble from his stomach accompanied his words. "I am so hungry my stomach is about to eat a hole in my backbone."

Magda was going through the packs, clucking worriedly. "Those Indians! They made such a mess that I can't find the coffee pot. Ah. There it is, wrapped in my only good petticoat! Ugh!

"But they did leave the food. I suppose they thought they'd take what they needed when it was necessary. And here is Mama's medical bag, thanks be to God!"

She took an armload of stuff and dropped it beside a bare patch where some large animal had wallowed away the grass. Johnny gathered dead branches beneath the trees, and a whisk or two of her flint and steel over her tinderbox had a blaze going with fair promptness.

Hot coffee and beans and cornpone, which Mama had learned from the Southerners among whom she had lived for so long, went down hastily, once she had them ready. Then Johnny scuffed out the fire and covered the ashes with loose dirt. He wanted no betraying smoke or glow to signal their position to anyone who might survive to follow them.

They had to sleep, whoever came behind them. For a time, their fates had to be left to chance, for another day of uninterrupted effort would see them both too exhausted to think clearly.

Johnny seemed to drop into a bottomless pit of darkness, relaxing totally for the first time since leaving Margarita's farm. But something woke him after a time, and he stared up into sunlit leaves overhead, listening hard. There came through the earth beneath his ear a familiar sound, and not a friendly one.

He sat abruptly and reached to touch Magda, but her eyes were open, her ear, too, pressed against the blanket that was flat to the ground. "Cavalry!" Her lips shaped the word without making a sound.

Johnny was on his feet, and she was up at once, helping him with rolling blankets, assembling packs, catching and saddling horses. He didn't whistle for the ponies, though they grazed some distance away in the edge of the grassland. He waited until one looked up and clicked his fingers, motioning for them to come. They flung up their heads, snorted, and came at once.

As the Gannellis moved their animals into a thick screen of brush on the other side of the creek, the jingle of bits and harness, the thud of hooves became audible. Johnny made certain that nothing could be seen of their horses, hiding them well beyond the water's edge in a thicket, and returned to a well concealed spot, from which he and Magda watched the land to north and east.

This was no rabble of raiders or independent band of Comanche. These were disciplined troops, riding with the unique rhythm of cavalry pacing itself for a long journey. A line of mounted men became visible, their shapes distorted by the heat rising from the soil as they headed into the setting sun toward the tree line.

Johnny had not intended to sleep away the entire day, but it was too late to worry now. These men were looking for a spot in which to camp for the night, and any attempt to ride away over the open grassland to the west would mean quick discovery. In Comanche country, everyone kept a sharp eye out in all directions.

He looked aside at Magda, and she quirked an eyebrow, watching the approaching troops with narrowed eyes. He could see by the faint flush rising in her olive face that she was remembering the last Yankee troops they had met.

He felt sudden pity for any cavalryman who might stumble over her. She was, as he found himself, ready to make more than a little trouble for such men, whether or not they had taken part in the Gannellis' downfall.

They moved back to their animals and made certain there was grazing within reach of their tethers. Magda remained with the mounts while Johnny slipped through the thickets toward the point at which he judged the troop would enter the trees.

He stopped short of the edge, taking refuge in a dense tangle of sawvines and hawthorn. There he made the best of his prickly location and waited to see what would come.

The jangles and clinks were near, now, and the sun was well down. Long shadows reached out across the rolling land to envelop the oncoming horses. The place toward which they headed was closer to the water than had been the one Johnny chose the night before. The trees were ranked so closely that he couldn't see the sky at all, when he looked straight up.

There came the crackle of dead leaves and branches beneath hooves, and men's voices muttered quietly. Then came the barked command, "*DIS*mount!"

Johnny knew with a shiver up his spine that his own small war was about to be reactivated. He moved back through the trees, grateful for the bustle of activity among the troops that would cover any slight noise he might make. Following the memorized route, he found Magda sitting on a root, talking softly in Italian to the ponies.

She looked up as he emerged from the bushes. "They're camped about a half mile farther along the creek. We need to take the horses to the western edge of the trees, all saddled and ready to go. Then we'll be set to hit those bastards hard and take off without wasting any time," he said.

She nodded. "I scouted out the woods on this side of the creek. There's a game trail that we can follow and the horses will make no sound to speak of. Come, I'll show you."

They found a stand of buckeye at the very edge of the trees, into which the horses blended without a trace. They hitched them, ponies and all, to the tough bushes and made ready to tackle their next task.

Magda was muttering under her breath as she checked her sleeves and her belt to make sure her knives were in position. Johnny did the same and moved away toward the Yankee camp.

He wondered about those men, so unsuspecting, feeling so safe in their numbers. That, if nothing else, was about to change.

CHAPTER FOURTEEN

By the time they reached the beaten-down area the troop had cleared for its camp, the group had settled in for the night. The pickets were in place, but Johnny and his cousin spotted them without any trouble and found ways to slip between their positions without too much difficulty.

Following brush tops and stumps, prickly growths of vines and bushes, they came at last to a spot from which they could see almost the entire encampment. There was a large cook fire over which the evening meal was being prepared. Three officers were drinking coffee poured from a tin pot in the edge of a smaller fire that had been built off to one side.

The night was too warm to need the heat, and the fires, Johnny knew, would be doused as soon as all the cooking was done.

The Yankees showed no signs of wariness. Even the pickets were less than alert. The officers had even slipped off their boots to ease their weary feet. From his hiding place, Johnny could hear their voices, even though they talked quietly.

"It's still a damn shame, Sir!" the lieutenant was saying, his sandy moustache bristling with emotion.

The officer, his back to Johnny, shrugged. "Fortunes of war," he said, though his tone did not sound philosophical. "No officer can lose an entire command, even to guerrillas, without expecting to pay for it.

"The court martial showed that my peers knew it did not reflect on my ability as a commanding officer when they found me not guilty, but they had to do something, once my wounds healed. Sending me to Fort Mason was what they decided on as punishment, and I know that has to be a hellhole, like the rest of this godforsaken place."

Against his shoulder, Magda stiffened, and Johnny knew why. That voice was hatefully familiar. This was their Captain, put into their path by what had to be the working of the Providence in which Mama had believed so devoutly.

Johnny turned his face to stare at his cousin. The firelight, filtered through intervening layers of leaves and branches, stippled her face, and her eyes gleamed almost red. He looked again at their prey, and they lay together, still as hunting cats.

After a time the fires were covered, and the pickets were relieved and replaced. Men and officers rolled into blankets and snores began punctuating the night. Still Johnny waited, motionless, for his instinct to tell him when it was time to move.

A screech owl tuned its wavering cry. Another, deeper among the trees, quavered a reply. Then Johnny moved toward the nearest of the pickets, sliding through the undergrowth like a snake.

* * * * * * *

Magda, waiting in their covert, heard no sound, but in a bit Johnny was beside her again. Now he smelled like blood, the coppery taint sharp on the night air.

She moved with him into the place where the officers were long lumps of darkness against the pale soil. The Captain lay on the farther side of the group, and Johnny went over to kneel beside the long shape.

Magda joined him, her hands moving quickly. When the Captain managed to wake, he was gagged, bound, and the two were carrying him swiftly into the woods.

She knew with sudden intuition that no nightmare in the man's life had ever been so terrible. He struggled, when he came to himself, but she held his feet tightly under her right arm, and Johnny had his hands hooked in the man's armpits, stretching his length between them so as to keep him from using his spine as a spring for getting loose.

When they were deep in the trees, they set his back against a tree trunk and stood, staring down at him in the dimness, for little starlight came through the overhead branches. She felt a smile begin to grow on her face, and Magda was glad Johnny could not see the fierce joy in her eyes.

She had thought Johnny insane when he tortured Hunk, back there in that horrible clearing. Now she knelt beside the Captain and said, knowing herself to be as mad as her cousin, "We meet again, Captain. You are the gentleman who hangs or shoots mountebanks, are you not? And here you are, in the hands of those you left for dead."

She glanced over her shoulder at Johnny. "What shall we do with him, *Caro Mio*?"

The man's eyeballs glinted faintly, so wide were his eyes. Johnny chuckled. "Not too much, as yet. We shall remind him of his past transgressions...yes. He seems to take no responsibility for his murders, and he feels, obviously, no guilt. Losing his command because of his own immoral decisions seems not to have made an impression on him.

"His spirit needs humbling, I think. We must drag it through the dust, just a bit, so that he can understand what will come next."

Magda felt a sudden nausea. "Johnny, surely you do not intend to do...that!...again." Her voice was tight in her throat.

"No, *Cara*. I find that I am not as appreciative of that art as the Comanche seem to be. I must find another way of entertaining our guest. Nothing painful, just humiliating. Let's begin by tying him to this convenient tree." His chuckle became a soft laugh.

"And remove his gag, when we are done? So that he will be forced to scream for help. That should be galling to that pride of his, do you not think?"

She found herself giggling with relief. "I should think so. Do you have enough rope with you?"

"Quite enough."

The Captain began squirming in his bonds, but they lifted him again and secured him against the bole of the tree. Johnny held him while Magda wound him tightly with the rope, tying it securely behind the trunk.

Her cousin moved. Her eyes now accustomed to the gloom, Magda saw him hold one wrist close to the Captain's eyes, and the faint glimmer of the stones in his wristlet came even to her eyes.

He scrubbed the leather against the stubbled cheek. "Feel this," said Johnny Gannelli. "I showed the wristlets to you, after you murdered our people. One day you will see these again, and on that day you will probably die.

"Remember that, my Captain. But for now we will leave you alive to dread the future."

Johnny bent to test the ropes. Magda knew that they were tight enough to make the man go numb. "Loose the gag, Cara," her cousin said. "Just enough so he can work it out with his tongue, given time."

She made sure that the gag was movable and rose to join Johnny. They slipped among the trees, their feet feeling for deadfall that might betray them to the remaining pickets.

Instead of heading toward their waiting horses, they made an arc, taking out all those standing guard around the encampment before firing a fusillade into the eastern edge and making tracks toward their mounts. They rode out in darkness, followed by the ponies and the packhorse. Blind shots on the other edge of the line of trees returned fire at a nonexistent foe.

Behind them, beyond the creek and the trees, there was a beehive-like disturbance, and they laughed as they cantered away. But the sound of more gunshots brought them up to turn their horses and stare eastward.

That sharp crackle came through the still air. Amid the cracks of the Army rifles they heard the deep boom of the large-bore that one of the bushwhackers had used in that other clearing against the Comanche.

Johnny stared at her in the starlight. "I wonder...." Magda completed his thought: "...if that is a surviving bandit or one of the Comanche who is firing that weapon. Did we lead them directly into that Yankee camp?"

Her cousin kicked his horse into motion. "However it happened, we are well out of it. The more they kill each other, the fewer there are for us to run away from or to fight, later. Come on, Mag. We are going west!"

* * * * * * *

Their small caravan moved at an easy lope that covered ground without tiring the mounts too much. Dismounting to rest the beasts slowed them a bit, but in time they reached wide open prairie country, without the frequent creeks and strips of woodland. They pushed on as dawn came, and at midmorning they paused in the lee of a small hill to make camp.

This was good grass country, Johnny decided, at least in spring. Their horses, hobbled, were loosed to graze, and they made no fire, chewing dried fruit and meat that Margarita had put into their packs many days before.

Magda insisted on watching while Johnny slept, and he made no protest, for his old wound was hurting like the devil. In a couple of hours he woke and took the watch while his cousin slept. He could detect no hint of pursuit, though he kept his gaze fixed toward the east. From time to time he put an ear to the ground, listening, but no vibration of a hoof came to him through the earth.

When Magda woke, they called the horses, saddled, and set out, carefully avoiding any column of smoke that might denote a farm or a campfire. Now they moved across land that rolled in long billows, low ridges covered with coarse grass, mesquite, and prickly pear. Once in a while they found a creek where willows grew, but there were few trees of any size except for the inevitable cottonwoods.

When they found such a watercourse, they filled their water bags, for Johnny had heard tales about the dry lands to the west. He didn't intend to be caught unprepared.

At sunset a new moon hung on the horizon, and they rode toward it in the early darkness. In the faint light, Johnny saw something stretching across the shallow valley ahead, cutting across their route at an angle.

"It looks like a road," said Magda. "Should we take that way to confuse the trail? It might be easier on the horses."

He grunted, undecided. He'd make up his mind when the time came, and he was no longer in a hurry. Surviving both Comanche and bushwhackers had given him a fatalistic attitude that left him alert and yet relaxed. Without a backward glance, he rode toward the angling road, content to wait before deciding.

Before dawn they had drawn near the track, and Magda agreed that it might be best to camp just out of sight of the road, near enough to know if anyone passed, but out of their range of vision. "I have a strange feeling," said Magda, busy with her blanket roll.

"I do, also," said Johnny. "Someone is following us, and I feel it strongly. Yet for some unlikely reason, I am not at all alarmed. How can you explain that?"

Magda made a wry face as she dropped onto her blanket and bit into a strip of dried fruit. "I can't. So let's just go to sleep and let come what will. Come Comanche or bushwhacker or Yankee cavalry, we can handle it, don't you think?"

He grinned and nodded. The dried stuff, tough but tasty, helped his growling belly, and he rolled himself into his blanket in a strange state of contentment. What more could happen to them, after all?

CHAPTER FIFTEEN

Before the last of the red dawn left the sky, Johnny was awake, sitting and listening. He hissed at Magda, who rolled over and opened her eyes.

"I heard the sound of hooves through the ground, but sitting I can't hear them any longer," he said.

Magda turned over and put her ear to the ground, lying very still as she listened to the sounds of morning earth. When she sat, her eyes were narrowed.

"You did hear them, but they are not near enough as yet. And I think they are not on the road. It is so close those would come through well. No, back to the east, I think, a horse comes this way. The one we have been waiting for? I wonder who that can be...?"

"Why wonder? Let's go and see," Johnny said, rising and beginning to set the packs in order and to call up the ponies, who were followed by the horses. In five minutes he was done, but they didn't mount up.

They moved like ghosts over the billows of land, heading eastward again, angling toward the direction from which they had come. From time to time one of them would drop to the ground and listen, and each time the sound of approaching hooves was more distinct.

Magda rose to her toes and pointed. "There!" she said. She was staring toward the dim line of trees on the horizon. "I see a horse, just one. Two men, one riding and one walking. The rider is slumped as if he is wounded. Can you see them?"

Johnny's eyes were not as sharp as his cousin's, but now he began to see what she described, picking out the shapes toward which she pointed. The sun helped, as he peered at the moving figures.

"Potesenaquahip," he said. "And Mugual. But there is nobody else that I can see. Look hard, Magda. Get on your horse so you will have more height."

She climbed onto her gray and stood in the stirrups, shielding her eyes and sweeping the grasslands with her penetrating gaze. But when she looked down she shook her head. "Nobody else."

Now the approaching walker had seen them. It was, without doubt, Mugual, his light young body easily distinguished from the heavier, taller one of Senaqua. He reached, as Johnny watched, to touch his companion on the knee, and the rider straightened a bit, glanced toward the watchers, and then slumped forward again.

"He's hurt badly," said Magda. She dismounted and began searching through one of the packs. "I will get the medicine bag. And over there is a good place to make a camp, out of the wind and out of sight of anyone traveling past."

She pointed toward a clump of scrub oak and mesquite under the roll of a rise. "I will get things ready there, while you go and help them to come in."

Johnny stared at his cousin, his mind whirling with speculation. "They're Comanche," he said. "They were going to abuse us terribly. Are you sure you want to do this?"

Magda snorted. "Senaqua saved us. He didn't want us tortured and killed, and he managed to get us out of there with all our supplies, without doing anything to hurt his own people at all. Old Horse Blanket or whatever they called the other chief was the one who held out against us.

"And Senaqua got us away. That tells me he is not only not as savage as he makes out, but also that he is extremely intelligent. Comanche or not, I'll help him. Better a Comanche than a Yankee, Cousin!"

Johnny began to nod. "And Mugual—I could just see him biting his tongue to keep from asking us to teach him trick riding and knife throwing. But he was too respectful of his elders to say anything." He moved away toward the approaching pair.

As he drew near them, it was plain that neither was alarmed by his appearance. Senaqua was lying along his horse's neck, his big strong body looking strangely flaccid. Mugual was holding onto him to keep him from sliding off entirely, and he looked up at Johnny with appeal hidden deep in his obsidian eyes.

"Here," said Johnny, coming up beside the other horse and easing Senaqua's weight onto his knee, then drawing him over onto his own mount, in the circle of his arms. "Mount his horse and come with me, Mugual. We'll attend to him." He glanced aside at the boy, now riding beside him. "What happened back there?"

He expected no reply, for Senaqua was obviously out of it at the moment. But Mugual, kicking his soft-shod heels into the flanks of the horse he rode, said, "We find soldier in trees. Have big fight. My father be shoot." He looked over at the limp man in Johnny's arms.

"I bring him away, after you. He no...."—He paused and thought hard for a moment, obviously searching for words in English to express his thought—"...no feel right with Comanche now. So I bring him. We be white men now."

Johnny laughed, heading out smartly toward the place where Magda waited. "It isn't quite that easy to become a white man," he said, "even if you're not an Indian. But why the hell not give it a try?"

When they pulled up the horses in the clump of scrub, Magda had a blanket spread in the shade, the medicine bag open, and Mama's bottle of medicinal whiskey and the other of laudanum ready for cleaning wounds and comforting the sufferer. She grinned at Mugual as the horses were loosed to graze with the others.

Johnny, favoring his own tender leg, lifted the wounded man down. The boy helped with his father, his hands strong and yet oddly gentle for one Johnny had been taught must be a savage, without tenderness for anyone.

Senaqua groaned faintly as they laid him on the blanket. His eyes opened, widening as he saw who bent over him, but he showed little surprise. His angular face was gray with loss of blood, but he showed no sign of the pain he was feeling.

Johnny knelt beside him and slid a knife blade through the blood-clotted thongs holding his deerskin shirt in place. The garment slid down, showing a mess of blood and the dark edges of wounds, already drying to brown.

"You don't have to keep on Injuning," Johnny said. "Mugual has decided that the two of you are going to be white men now. Might as well practice moaning and groaning and bitching about things that don't suit you. Start turning loose of your civilized habits; to be a real white man you have to lie and cheat and kill, while telling yourself it's the only right thing to do. Learn to be a ring-tailed twister, if it seems to be the profitable route."

The Comanche almost chuckled, but caught himself in time as a spasm of pain gripped him. He settled for a thin-lipped grin. "It is not necessary for you to lesson me in that sort of thing. Do you forget that I have lived with the white-eyes for many years?"

Magda raised her head and said, "Be still! I've got to get all that lead out of you, and if you talk, it makes you wiggle. Just hush and let me get on with this. You may enjoy being mined for lead, but I was not cut out to be a miner."

Senaqua quirked a brow at Johnny, who shrugged. Incipient white man or not, the Indian lay motionless, soundless, as the girl removed the slugs from his body, three from his torso, two from the left upper arm, and one from his right thigh, just below the hip.

She doused the wounds with whiskey and began bandaging, while Johnny held up the dark head and poured a swallow of laudanum into the Comanche's mouth. Some of the wounds were gaping ones, and those she stitched with Mama's mending supplies, then wrapped them well and tightly to prevent more bleeding.

"You must have done something right," she muttered as she finished. "Any one of these should have bled you to death, if they had been a hair nearer an artery. As it is, you're going to be stiff as a board and sore all over for a long time, but you will live a while, still."

"I would not guarantee that," Senaqua said. "Mugual and I, we are not going back to the Comanche. There is no point in that, for our race is dying before our eyes. I know, if the boy does not, that white men shoot first and inquire into right and wrong later, if they trouble to do it at all. I have no objection to dying; that is something anyone can learn to do well. But I do hate wasting what is left of my life in hunting a dead buffalo."

"We want to go west," said Johnny. "And that damned Captain will be on our heels, if he is still alive. If you were able to travel, we'd take you with us."

"Why do we have to go west?" asked Magda. "We just picked that out of a hat, so to speak. Why not go south and east? There is wooded land there, with plenty of water. Game and fish and growing things.

"If we must be fugitives, then why be fugitives in country where there is little cover and water is so scarce that a watched waterhole may mean that you are taken captive? I heard the people in Arkansas talking about the lands in eastern Texas.

"Many had family who emigrated there, and they envied them. The Captain expects us to head west. Why not go east and south instead?"

Johnny was thinking hard about her words. Why *not* go southeast? With Senaqua and Mugual, they would be a different party from the one the Captain would be searching for. And, down there in the more settled part of the state, there would be Yankees to torment.

"How would you like to enlist in my army?" he asked Senaqua.

The Comanche had been lying still, eyes closed. Now he opened a black slit of eye and looked up, skeptically. "I was only in what might be called the army of my people because I was born into the tribe. Ours is a system in which one usually does as he pleases, no matter what chiefs say. Organized armies, as I have observed them, are not the sort of thing I enjoy."

"This is going to be a freehand, freelance, do-it-yourself army," Johnny answered. "More like the way your people wage war than like the cavalry does, believe me." He looked at his cousin, and she nodded, her dark eyes sparkling with mischief.

"We can go down into those big woods, with plenty of water and game and such, and there will be no supply problem at all, except for ammunition. We'll take that, with weapons, from the Yankees, and we'll give the blue-coats hell, six ways from sundown. The four of us should be able to deal them some misery, if we put our minds to it, once you get well. And if we're smart about it, they may never know how many of us there are, much less *who* we are."

Senaqua turned his head and spoke in gutturals to his son. Mugual's eyes glittered with excitement, though he kept his face straight.

Then Senaqua said, "It does sound interesting. Just our sort of thing, in fact. A lot of tiny wars, hit and run, we shall be what my Spanish acquaintances call *guerrillas*. Once I am able to move about, of course."

"Don't try to deceive me," said Johnny. "You could rise from that blanket and do a war dance right now, if you wanted to. But for heaven's sake, don't try it. Just rest, while we sit around and talk about all the ugly things we intend to do to the Yankees down there in East Texas."

But the Indian seemed ready to talk. "I have traveled in that country, though my people seldom go so far east. I came through by that route, and I was amazed at the dense forest and the plentiful water. My people are used to open country with few trees, but there you can travel for days without seeing the sun. Mud-bottomed creeks and sloughs lead to mud-colored rivers that run southeastward through the woodlands."

"No wonder so many people have gone there to live," said Magda.

The Indian laughed. "I was there in August, and it was a wet month, which I was told that it seldom is. The heat was thick and muggy enough to choke you. Our heat is dry; there it is like being under a steaming wet blanket. Many who lived there wished they had remained in Tennessee or Mississippi. Most have malaria. For every hardship escaped by settling in wet country, you find at least one that you did not expect."

Johnny stretched his long legs and leaned against his blanket roll. He laughed. "We probably will not live long enough to have to worry about malaria. The Yankees, we have found, are a much more fatal sickness.

"Yet this seems to be the right thing to do; we are not equipped for a very long journey through bad country. We have no money to buy anything, if we could risk going into a town after supplies.

"If any of those back there are still alive and the Captain is capable of activity, we are going to be a popular target of northern troops, from the Red River to the Rio Grande. There will, I suspect, be wanted posters too, for I imagine that bastard took some of Papa's circus posters for our likenesses. Papa put several up in the towns we went through."

Magda yawned. "I am going to take another nap. We can't travel right now with Senaqua in this condition. And when it gets dark, you are going to want to move. We have half a day to rest before we begin moving eastward."

She turned toward Senaqua, and he turned his dark gaze toward her. "You go to sleep. You are going to need all that stiff upper lip when we start out. Rest while you can." She lay flat on the brittle grass and closed her eyes.

Mugual squatted patiently beside his father, and Johnny leaned harder against his blanket roll. Magda was right, as usual. When night came, he intended to have his party of ill-assorted companions on the move toward their goal. They might go slowly and pause frequently, but they would not be sitting ducks for anyone who came looking for them.

He closed his own eyes, feeling the sun warm against his shoulders, and drifted away into sleep.

CHAPTER SIXTEEN

The next morning Potesenaquahip and Mugual finished telling about their skirmish with the Yankees, which had been both quick and hot, resulting in the scattering of the Comanche. Johnny had a strong hunch they should move from their present location.

This road seemed to be a well used north-south track, which the troops coming from the northeast would probably intend to use. And the Captain would now, he felt certain, be on the lookout for both Indians and Gannellis.

Magda protested. "If we move Senaqua, he's going to bleed even more. Even a Comanche will eventually run out of blood. We need a place well off any trail, sheltered, with a source of water. And I would suggest moving east, for they said they are going south and west."

Senaqua, who had been listening with his eyes closed, nodded. He grunted a long string of gutturals toward Mugual, who stood and looked off to the east as if he saw something invisible to the eyes of the whites.

Senaqua turned his head and motioned in the direction in which his son was staring. "There is a house out there, a half day's ride perhaps, or a full day's crawl at the pace I can endure.

"Once a farm was there. It was...visited...by our warriors, and now there is only the house." His face was expressionless. "No one was left to take word of the fate of the family to any other whites, and we sometimes find a use for the shelter."

Johnny shivered to think what had happened to the tenants of that house. He straightened and shrugged. "It sounds ideal," he said. He tried not to picture the sufferings of those who had lived there.

Magda was looking at him, but he didn't turn to meet her gaze. She was thinking just what he thought, for they knew each other too well and had shared their lives for too long for him to be mistaken about that.

Already she was getting up and putting the packs together. Mugual, without being told, brought the horses. Johnny whistled for the ponies, and they came at a gallop. In a few moments they were ready to move the wounded man.

That was easy, for Senaqua forced his weakened body onto the horse with no complaint and lay along its neck again, with Mugual riding one of the ponies alongside to steady him. Johnny led his horse into the approaching night, the new moon behind him in the west.

Ahead the land rolled more deeply, and before full dark he could see a faint haze on the horizon that had to be trees. They rode all night, by starlight and the faint light of the moon. They crossed a river, now low in its sandy banks, the water muddy, but they watered the horses and rested the wounded man in its deep cut.

Dawn was touching the sky ahead of them when they moved out of a shallow valley, over a low ridge, and saw before them the roof of a house, a pale patch of gray against the dark growth now covering most of the countryside. Trees and bushes grew in a tangle about the place, Johnny saw as he drew near, and the narrow porch leaned away from the wall, touching the ground at one end.

They pulled up in a clump of brush and watched the house before going in. A fox yipped in the shrubbery, and night birds twittered, disturbed, as they waited for Mugual to scout the position. But the boy returned as silently as he went, motioning for them to proceed.

Johnny took care not to disturb the vines and bushes as they made their way into the gaping front door, carrying Senaqua between himself and Mugual. He had noted the quiet trickling of water as they waited, and he knew a spring must water the area, very near the house.

Frogs and crickets were still chorusing in the thick growth, and he suspected that the water supply would be ample. This was a perfect place for a home. What a pity that it had proved so deadly for those who built it.

The interior of the big room was dry-rotted, musty, and cluttered with random debris. "How long has this place been empty?" Johnny asked Senaqua.

"Mugual was a small child when last we came here. Perhaps fifteen years." A fine line appeared between the dark brows. "I was still unhappy with my memories of white men's ways. Now I am older and understand that every sort of person has his own shortcomings, but then I was less tolerant of any failings except my own." He sighed.

Magda was moving about, brushing the trash aside with a bundle of twigs. Now she halted, staring at the wall behind a curtain of cobweb. "Explain this for me, if you can," she said.

Johnny came to peer at the spot she indicated. There the wall was covered with drawings done in chalky white. They were of horses, drawn in primitive style but quite recognizable, and of men with guns.

The entire space was filled with action: battles, pursuits, men lying dead on the ground. While the art was not sophisticated, it had its own sort of vigor.

Mugual looked, went back to his father and muttered into his ear. Senaqua laughed, holding his chest together with both hands. "My people draw," he said, "and white men's walls are long and smooth. There is a soft white rock they use to make the lines. I have no idea why they draw only horses and men with guns, but it is always so. Others of my kind must have camped here over the years."

"Not for a long time, by the look of the cobwebs," Magda said. She turned at the nicker of a horse. "But outside there is plenty of grazing for the animals. I will go and hobble them, while Johnny builds a fire in the fireplace. There is, heaven knows, plenty of wood here."

It was a perfect hideout for a healing man. For days they rested there, feeding Senaqua as well as the remains of their supplies would allow, and, once they were depleted, catching fat rabbits in snares and simmering them with wild onions and corn from volunteer stalks in the long abandoned garden into a nourishing stew.

Senaqua was able to ride at dusk of the final day, and they stole over the low ridge into a skimpy wood of scrub-oak and elm. The horses were reluctant to leave the lush grass and stamped and sidled, shaking their heads, but the riders forced them on, and the ponies trotted after them.

Johnny found that the trees grew larger as they moved eastward and to the south. Now forest began bulking large against the sky, and there were fewer glades and more creeks, all running roughly southeast. The deeper they went into East Texas, the better Johnny found himself liking it.

Before midnight, they had covered some eight miles or so. This was not as far as he would have liked, but it was better than expected, given Senaqua's condition. The moon was higher, and by its light they made fairly good time.

After midnight's time for rest, they started out again, Mugual going ahead as usual. After an hour or so he reappeared on foot and stopped Johnny, who was in the lead. "Smoke," he said. "Fire out, still smell smoke."

Johnny, straining his senses, smelled it too, faint and acrid on the night air. "Someone camping upwind of us?" he asked.

They all listened, motionless except for the occasional stamp or swish of a horse's tail. After some time, Senaqua said, "I heard a horse snort. And something has been cooked over that fire and probably is still in the pot. That is not the Indian way. I think it is not the way of the soldiers, either."

"Let's go and see," said Magda. "We can just follow our noses. I'd rather know who is there than worry about who it might be."

Why not? Johnny turned his mount's nose toward the wind, and the others fell in behind. They angled northward from their original course, the scent growing stronger as they moved. After a short while, Mugual stopped his pony and slid to the ground again, and they dismounted.

They went very cautiously through the brush, moving until they could see into a small clearing. In its middle, sparks were visible where a fire had blazed, and the smell of stew was plain on the cool air. The pot still sat in the ashes.

Something darker than its background bulked at the farther side of the clearing. He touched Senaqua, who straightened with some effort and peered into the gloom.

"A wagon," said Johnny. "Yes. And everyone asleep." The Comanche's tone held disgust. "If we were a raiding party, they would all be dead."

"Not on your tintype!" said a gruff voice behind them. Johnny, his heart in his throat, whirled, but the scrub was dark and thick, and nobody was visible.

"Just don't get too uppity. I'd hate to have to see what a load of buckshot would do to you at this distance. It'd make mincemeat out of the lot of you. Now go right ahead, one at a time, into the clearing. Slowly."

Johnny, his hands held high, did as ordered, and he heard the others coming behind, Senaqua's breath coming harshly as he was helped along by Magda and his son.

"Put your weapons on the ground. And don't claim you're unarmed, because anybody out here without guns would be too addled to walk straight. Hassie Mae!" The voice bellowed so suddenly that Johnny jumped.

Another voice, soft and light, came from the right. "Yes, Ma'am. I've got them in my sights."

That had to be a lie, but Johnny didn't feel up to putting it to the test. Besides which, Number One, with that shotgun, was still behind him. He heard solid footsteps crackling in the deadfall on the ground.

He took his pistol from its makeshift holster, and laid it beside the rifles and the small shotgun that Margarita had given Magda. He left his knives in his sleeves, knowing that his cousin had done the same. Whoever these people might be, they wouldn't find his group completely helpless.

Something went *scritch!* and light bloomed in a lantern globe. A young woman stepped forward, holding the light aloft with one hand and keeping a rifle, which looked longer than she was tall, trained steadily upon them. The thing was a flintlock, but it was undoubtedly loaded and primed, and she held it as if she knew what to do with it.

"Well, that's better. Let's get a look at you," said the gruff voice. "By golly, a mixed lot if I ever saw one!" A dumpy little woman came out of the scrub and stared at them, her shotgun in a relaxed grip that promised lightning alertness.

"And who might you be? And why are you sneaking around my camp in the middle of the night? Stealing horses? A bit of rape and plunder? Speak up!"

For once, Senaqua seemed speechless. Johnny sighed and began, "I am Johnny Gann. This is my sister Maggie, and these are our friends. Potesenaquahip and Mugual are father and son and more civilized than they look. We are going down into East Texas to make war on the Yankees."

This was too bald a statement, and he hadn't intended to make it, but it was too late to change that now.

"Oho!" she snorted. "Holdout Rebs?" Her voice was too guileless.

"Hell, no," Johnny said. "They could kill each other off, and I wouldn't shed a tear. The Yankees killed our family, and the Rebels took all our horses before that. I have no use for either side.

"We did a little evening up with the Yankees who killed our folks, and that got us into trouble. So we decided that if we had to be outlaws, we'd go all the way and become guerrillas."

He gestured toward the two Comanche. "These two have volunteered for our little army. They don't like either side, either." He looked straight into her faded gray eyes, and the lamplight showed him a lined, worn face that held more than a touch of humor.

"You go ahead and shoot us, if you decide that is best. Or let us go about our business. We just wanted to know who was camped so near us and to see if they might pose a danger to our party."

Hassie Mae set her lantern on the tailgate of the wagon and sat down beside it. She began laughing, a note of hysteria in her voice. "There you are, Ma. I told you there had to be a Providence, didn't I? And here we get an army all ready to get to work, just delivered right to our doorstep. I swear, it even surprises me, and I never doubted that something would happen.

"It just goes to prove that God don't care whether you believe in Him or not. When he's got a mind to, He'll take a hand, even if the person He helps is one who'd spit in His eye."

The old woman stared at the girl for a long moment. Then she turned to look her captives over, this time taking great pains to give them her entire attention.

"You're sure as hell not farmers. Not shopkeepers, even broke ones. I know most kinds of people and most kinds of trades, but I don't ever recall seeing anybody quite like the pair of you," she said, as she surveyed the Gannellis.

Magda cocked a brow in Johnny's direction. He grinned and held his hands at shoulder height. His cousin, some five paces distant, took two steps and launched herself into the air, coming to a stop palm-to-palm with Johnny, upside down, her slender body straight, her toes pointed daintily toward the stars.

"By God!" said the woman. "Circus folks! But it's been quite a ways back, from the look of you. And you two...."—she turned her gaze toward Senaqua and his son, standing stoically in the dimness—"...probably have been givin' Yankees hell too, eh?"

Senaqua nodded, his black eyes bright as coal in his seamed face.

"And you are all goin' off, calm as you please, to take on the U.S. government, in all its glory." She sounded as pleased and wondering as a child on Christmas morning.

"Well, I have a deal for you. You add Hassie Mae and me to your roster of troops. You have just enlisted Ma Devinney and Hassie Mae Harper. Now sit down and let me stir up that fire. There's stew enough left, if we skimp a little." She bustled about, pushing broken sticks into the scanty coals.

"We need to talk a little before we take off tomorrow. I've got stuff in that wagon that would make your hair stand on end, haven't I, Hassie Mae? Things that can make your line of work easier by a long shot."

The girl nodded, already stirring the sticky remains of the stew, now cooked firmly to the pot.

Stunned by this sudden addition to his troop, Johnny sat beside the fire, now beginning to crackle as fresh sticks were added. The bowl of warm stew might be a tad scorched, and the spoon he held might not be the cleanest he ever saw, but the food was comforting to his stomach.

As he ate, he thought. Somehow, he was sure, he would find good use for Ma Devinney and her soft-spoken companion.

CHAPTER SEVENTEEN

They decided that, traveling together with Ma's wagon, the group would be unidentifiable as the fugitives from an Arkansas circus and a Texas Indian fight. They might seem odd and hard to categorize, but certainly they shouldn't rouse the suspicion that the Gannellis or the two Comanche would on their own.

After settling that, they slept for a time, but everyone woke after a few hours and was ready to rise, though it was far from daylight still. Ma Devinney built up the fire again and they gathered in the firelight to continue their discussion.

As Johnny filled in the story of the death of the Gannelli Family Circus, he could see a spark of interest in the old woman's eyes. She paid equal attention to the Comanche's account, delivered in precise English that came as a shock from one who seemed to be a skin-clad savage.

At last their tales were done, and Ma poked up the fire and cleared her throat. She set a chew of tobacco into her cheek, spat twice, and began.

"There's been Devinneys running the boarding house in Alatosa, Louisiana, since the Lord knows when. It's the only place to stay in forty miles, any direction, and the main road goes right spang through the town, what there is of it which isn't much.

"My husband's granddaddy built the house, and the family added on as time went on, for it was a good business and kept the entire clan busy. When I married Ab, his folks was still tolerable young, able to take care of the place, so Ab and me took up a piece of creek bottom land and farmed for a while." She spat into the fire, sending a bright sputter of sparks into the air.

"We had four children just as fast as the law allowed and not one lived long enough to be weaned. We was some discouraged, as you might guess, but about that time Ab's Daddy died. His Ma needed us to help her with the boardinghouse, and that was something different to do.

"It took us away from the farm and kept us from thinking about all the dead babies. We never looked back, after that, just dived in and did a bang-up job of the thing."

Hassie Mae leaned over and put a small hand on Ma's work-roughened fingers in silent sympathy, but the old woman shook her head and went on. "We mainly put up timber cruisers and the schoolteacher and travelers going through to Shreve's Port where the ferry crossed the river. There was lots of folks coming over here to Texas, all the time, and we got along real well." She sighed, rubbing her wedding ring absentmindedly.

"We thought the whole thing about the War was crazy. We never owned slaves; nobody we knew except the Le-Doziers did either, and they were turning theirs loose and giving them land along the river, after the old man died.

"We didn't intend to stick our noses into any part of that mess, and we never suspected that people who'd known us since we was babies would take out after us the way they did. A big patriotic Confederate movement got started, and when it was plain that Ab and me didn't want to join it, they *hung* my husband, right in front of me and his Ma.

"It wasn't our neighbors that done it, make no mistake. A bunch of fired-up recruits come through Alatosa and got halfway drunk in our local saloon. They asked if there was anybody in town that needed to be encouraged to be a patriot, and some fool mentioned Ab." She was pale, even in the firelight, and her fingers clenched in her lap.

"Those bastards come charging up and hauled him out of the dining room. They beat him up, with his Ma and me held off at gunpoint.

"When he wouldn't give in and join up, they hung him right there on our own front porch, with the rocking chairs going like crazy from the shaking of the floorboards. Not one of our friends and neighbors said a word to save him."

"So that's why you haven't any use for the boys in gray," said Magda. "I do not blame you."

Ma grunted. "Ab's Ma and me, we just gritted our teeth and kept on running the boardinghouse. Hired Hassie Mae here to help out, being as there wasn't any boys left around to tend the horses and such. Just as well...Hassie can outdo any two boys ever born."

The girl blushed and drew back from the fire. Johnny wondered if anyone could be quite as timid as Hassie Mae seemed.

But Ma Devinney had not finished her tale. "So the War went on and on and on, and things got really tight. Nobody had a dime of cash money. With the men gone, crops were scanty, and it got hard to find anything to cook for the boarders, much less for us. We were wore out with the whole notion, by the time word came about Appomattox.

"And then the damn Yankees come riding into Alatosa." She frowned, her small pale eyes disappearing into her wrinkles. "They clumped into my clean hall without wiping the horse dung off their boots. Wanted this and wanted that, and treated us like we was varmints instead of people.

"They thought they'd make free with Hassie Mae, too, but she stuck a pitchfork into the rump of one of the sergeants, and that got their hackles up." She spat again, and Hassie Mae withdrew entirely into the shadows.

"They ate everything we had, messed up everything else, and saddled up to go. For a farewell present, they set fire to the house.

"By the time they left, there wasn't a thing there but hot coals. They sat there on their horses and wouldn't let a soul go near or do so much as throw water on the place or try to get anything out, after Ab's Ma give a screech and run back in with a bucket of water off the porch, and the roof caved in on her."

A wicked grin stole across the seamed features. "But Hassie and me had the old horse back in the pasture. He was too wore out for either army to steal. And we had Ab's store of blasting powder and caps that he used to blow stumps out of the new ground we used to farm. He'd stored it dry and tight, and while it ain't what you might call safe, it ain't near as dangerous as you'd think.

"I calculate it's still good, and I intend to blow some Yankees to Kingdom Come with it, if I can figure out how to do it. I figure if they hadn't started tryin' to tell us how to run our own business, there never would've been a war in the first place, so they're the ones to blame, when you get right down to it."

Johnny stared at her, his mind racing. "You have explosives, traveling right in the wagon with you?" He felt possibilities racing through his mind. "Consider yourself enlisted in my army, Ma. I never thought I'd get anything like that without having to take it away from the troops."

"Got it all packed in with straw around it. Old quilts from the house on the farm keep it fairly cool in hot weather, and we put feather pillows under it to soften the jolts. Nobody looking at the pile would guess it's anything but some bug-bit bedding.

"Hassie and me always intended to make our objections felt, if we ever got the chance. We needed a general, though, and now it looks as if we've found one."

Senaqua grunted. Johnny turned to look into his black eyes, and he found the Comanche laughing, in that still faced Indian manner of his. "Just by coincidence," he said in his deep voice, "my second owner was a mining engineer. He used explosives often, in the course of his work, and he allowed me to carry it to his sites.

"I watched him set his charges, and I know how he fused them and set them off. I am by way of being the nearest thing you have to an explosives expert, though a true professional would never consider me that. What skill I learned, however, is at your service."

Johnny drew a long breath. He had no clear idea what he intended to do. He had assumed that opportunities for harassment would occur, and that he and Magda would deal with them as they came up. Now, before his eyes, a coherent campaign was taking shape. Down in those well watered forestlands it would be simple to stay in hiding between forays. Probably, there would be a lot of disgruntled Confederates who were ready to lend a hand, too.

His only regret was that his pet Captain was heading off in another direction. Of course, after his encounter with the Comanche he might not be alive; yet Johnny still had a strong hunch that he would meet the man again.

He grinned across the fire at Magda. She was staring into the coals, her expression enigmatic. Ma Devinney was looking at Senaqua quizzically, and Hassie Mae was keeping an apprehensive eye on both the Comanche.

He nodded to Senaqua. "I think we are about to go to war, my friends. Seriously and effectively. Are you all quite willing? I would not want to draft anyone into so dangerous an enterprise without their consent."

One by one the heads nodded. Then Ma slapped her hand to her mouth and gasped.

"By God!" she croaked, "I forgot about Luke. There's still another one of us, if you want him!"

"The more the merrier," said Johnny, wondering what new surprise the old woman was about to spring.

CHAPTER EIGHTEEN

Hassie Mae began laughing. "Lord, Ma, we'd forget our heads if they weren't stuck on tight. I have to admit it. I forgot about him, too. I'll go wake him up right now. Not that the poor critter will do us much good, but we wouldn't want to draft him into our army without he says so."

She rose and turned, her long, drab skirts swirling around her legs and outlining a good figure. "I'll just be a minute."

"Who is Luke?" Johnny asked Ma.

She shrugged. "He's a piece of scrap left over from the War," she said. "He floated into our path, and we couldn't stand to leave him behind. You'll see what I mean in a minute. I don't rightly know how to explain the way he is, and I haven't a notion what he used to be."

Johnny waited, watching the fire, hearing the comforting crackle amid the early morning sounds of birds waking in the woods. Owls hooted in the distance, and frogs and crickets made a racket beside the creek at the bottom of the slope.

Hassie Mae returned, after a bit, and said, "He's coming. I hated to wake him. He's a little addled right now, but when he comes to real well he's pretty bright. You just have to work at him."

Turning, Johnny saw motion beside the dim shape of the wagon, which was outside the circle of firelight. There was an awkward shape crawling out, and it stood uncertainly, wavering on legs that seemed less than dependable. Then it moved toward the fire, swinging along on one rude crutch and one leg. The other ended just about the knee.

When Luke hobbled into the light, Johnny saw that he was what remained of a tall, strong man. But his shoulders were already warping to the stress of the crutch, and his face, clean shaven, held defeat in every line.

The man found a chunk of wood the right height and levered himself down, laying his crutch beside him. He stared about the circle of strange faces with some bewilderment, his black eyes startled and his expression disoriented.

"What the blue-eyed hell is going on here?" he asked, his voice a deep boom. His accent was almost as refined as Senaqua's. This had been a gentleman, Johnny realized, before he became a wreck.

Ma handed him a tin cup of coffee, and he handled it gingerly, padding the hot sides with a dirty bandanna. "These folks are going to start their own little war with the Yankees, Luke," she said. Her weathered face looked almost gentle as she gazed at him.

"They've got reasons just about as good as yours and mine, too. Hassie and me have just enlisted, but we mighty near forgot about you." She spat another stream of brown tobacco juice into the fire. "Seems to me you've got as much grudge against 'em as anybody I know, though you've never told us a word about what happened to you. Might be you'll want to enlist, but if not, there's no hard feelings."

He gazed around the group, his dark eyes unreadable. He checked off Johnny, Magda, and the pair of Comanche. No surprise altered his expression, as he sipped the hot coffee. When he had finished his survey, he drained the cup and laid it on the ground beside him.

"You have your reasons, I do not doubt," he said. "Without any doubt, I have mine, which I consider sufficient. Where do you intend to carry out your unofficial hostilities?" His hands, long and bony, clenched in the shadow of his body, but Johnny saw and knew that this was a man filled with rage.

"We're heading for the forested country to the south and east. There's plenty of water and lots of cover," Johnny said.

"Intelligent choice," Luke replied. "And you intend, I suspect, to make use of the explosive Mrs. Devinney has hidden in her wagon?"

Potesenaquahip laughed, a single humorless bark. "I will have that honor," he said.

Luke turned to stare into those obsidian eyes. "A highly unusual assortment of talents," he said, his tone wry. "And what does the young lady do in this endeavor?"

Moved by some obscure impulse, Magda flipped three knives out of her sleeves and spun them to stick into the block of wood on which the one-legged man was sitting. The motion was so quick that her hands hardly seemed to move.

Luke blinked rapidly, though he kept his face expressionless. Even when Magda rose and walked on her palms toward Johnny, then flipped to stand in the palms of his hands, the man seemed unperturbed.

"I take it that you are circus folk."

Johnny nodded.

"Useful talents, I do not doubt," Luke mused. "Though highly unorthodox. I take it that you do trick riding? Wriggle your way into and out of positions that would tie normal spines into knots? Swing through the air fearlessly and hurl yourselves into space?"

"We can." Now Johnny was beginning to feel wary. This was not the war-ravaged ruin of a man that he had expected to find. "What can *you* do?"

There came a long pause. Luke seemed to be debating, inside himself, how much to reveal to these new associates. Then, with a what-the-hell shrug, he spoke.

"I can shoot the eye out of a gnat at a hundred paces. Put me into a spot where I am solidly braced and do not have to move, and I can lay down a field of fire that will keep all enemy heads down. Some permanently." And now there was emotion in those eyes, adding its own bitter tinge to their dark depths.

In his turn, Johnny said, "A highly useful talent. Have you any more?"

"I can think, coolly and effectively, under any possible circumstances. When I want desperately to become unconscious or drunk out of my head, I still think with precision and logic." His laugh was almost a groan.

"I have also acquired strength in my arms and hands, since my unfortunate misunderstanding with a Union slug and the even more unfortunate encounter with a Yankee surgeon."

"I take it that you are in sympathy with our aims?" Johnny asked him. "Are you willing to go with us into the woods and wreak havoc upon our enemies, who are experienced and disciplined troops capable of wiping us out?"

Luke took up his cup and held it out to Ma Devinney, who filled it from the smoke-blackened pot. "I was once a cautious man," he said. "Even a timid one, you might say, when it came to risky enterprises. I was a careful husband, a careful father, a careful custodian of my family's properties. I was even, as far as possible, a careful soldier. Much good did it do me! I lost everything—land, home, wife, children, and leg. Along with those I lost every bit of my caution.

"Now I am a reckless man with nothing left to lose. You may enlist me in your tatterdemalion army, if you think you might use one of my limited talents."

Ma's gaze was fixed on Luke, and her mouth was half open, her eyes filled with disbelief. "Luke, what's come over you? You're a long shot from being the man who crawled into the back of that wagon last night."

He smiled. The defeated lines tracking his face were disappearing. The lines that remained were those of wear and suffering, but they also had a trace of hope among their traceries.

"I must beg your forgiveness, Ma. When you found me, I was just what you saw, a shattered man, almost mindless with grief. I cared for nothing, thought about nothing. I accepted your care and kindness without giving anything back to you. It frightened me to think that anyone would learn who I was, deep inside where the capacity for pain still existed." He straightened his back and set his hand squarely on the abruptly ended knee.

"I had no hope of ever being able to change my state of mind or body, until these unlikely angels came along to offer me a chance." He sighed. "You cannot offer to return to me what I have lost. Not even real angels could do that. But you offer me vengeance, and that is far better than nothing. If I can send some Bluebellies to Hell it will comfort my soul."

"So here we have the nucleus of a hit-and-run group," said Johnny. Too much pain had been carried on Luke's voice to allow any stillness to follow them. His own voice drowned that agony.

"We have a wagon with explosives, compliments of Ma Devinney and Hassie Mae. We have a sharpshooter in Luke here. We have an explosives expert. We have an excellent horse-handler in Mugual, and probably an even better horse thief." He looked at Mugual, and the boy's eyes glittered in the firelight. He nodded, one sharp dip of his chin.

"We have two knife-throwers, acrobats, trick riders, and all-around spies in Maggie and me. That should be enough to begin with. Even the Union Army might shiver to think that such an unexpected force was going to be dogging its stragglers."

Hassie Mae cleared her throat. "You have somebody who can go into town and find out things, too. I'll never be suspected. I'm not a fugitive, and I look respectable. I can cover for you even better than Ma, because she never learned to keep her temper, bless her. In me you have a contact woman who can be your link with other people. If you want one, that is."

Johnny laughed, this time with true gladness. "You are entirely correct. We do need such a link, and we also need every clear head we have. I think we possess a prime collection, here around this fire.

"But now we had better rest, for I take it that we are agreed to go east tomorrow? Or today, for it is only a couple of hours until sunrise."

"I got most of a night's sleep," said Luke. "I shall sit here and watch, while the rest of you take a nap, if you like. I need to pull myself together again into some sort of effective human being."

By the time Johnny had seen their mounts secured, their packs unloaded, it was early light. Still, he insisted that they sleep for a few hours before Luke called them to the breakfast he volunteered to cook.

It was almost time to put their campaign on the road.

CHAPTER NINETEEN

They moved into the morning as the sun rose hot behind the trees. It was now clear that the land was rolling
into deeper valleys and higher hills as they angled toward
the southeast. From time to time they came out into hilltop
clearings, obviously the work of fires, and Johnny could
see at last a forest of old pines, rising tall and deeply green
from the river bottom country below his position.

Luke stumped up beside him as he stood in the shade
of a hickory tree, resting his horse. "It's funny how you
never find pine trees farther west than a certain point.
They just stop, as if someone had put up a signpost, saying, "All pines keep out!"

He leaned against the hickory, scratching his chin with
the top of his crutch. "In time you will come to value those
trees, for they give good shelter for livestock in winter,
and pine straw is the best possible flooring for a tent.
Where we are going, the woods are mostly pine, in some
spots, and the one I have in mind is one of those. It should
suit our purposes well."

Ma Devinney was rehitching the spavined horse,
which had been loosed to graze and drink from a bucket of
water during the rest stop. She kept glancing at Luke as if
she couldn't believe he was the same person she'd nursed
back to health.

"I can't get over it," she said. "That's no more the Luke Cornwall I picked up out of the road than you are. It's a pure D miracle."

Hassie, coming around the wagon, said, "You can't see yourself, Ma. You look ten years younger than you did two days ago. When these folks came, we were just batting around blind. Now we know what we're going to try to do. I think it's because we feel there's a reason to go on living. Even if that reason is just killing Yankees. Never in the world did I think I'd turn out to be an outlaw, but then I hadn't been through a war. That will make anybody turn bad, just in self defense."

The horses were ready to travel again, and it was time to take off into that rolling green sea. Johnny felt his chest tighten with excitement or perhaps it was apprehension. Yet he felt it was more like homecoming, even though most of his life had been spent in country somewhat different from this. As he mounted, the wristlet on his right wrist caught the light, and the quiet gems sparked, sending a knife of pain through his heart.

The old life—sudden nostalgia swept over him, a longing for the simple routines of practice and performance and scrounging for food for both people and animals. Then swinging free above the ring with Magda in his grip or the solid slap of the trapeze bar into his hands...those were in his blood, inherited from generations of his forebears, and that Captain had wiped it all out in one blind evening of murder.

He felt hot, as he turned his mount to follow the wagon down the rough track into the trees. It would be a while, but when he began, he would wipe out some of the bitterness, he hoped.

He felt Magda staring at his back and smiled. She knew, he didn't doubt, what he was thinking.

The forest closed over their heads, and except for occasional glades where fires or tornados had cleared away the trees, it was like moving through a tremendous hall in some dim cathedral. The pines, as they traveled, became taller, wider in girth, until at last they were moving along smooth straw between columns which, at the butt, must have been far wider than the wagon bed.

He watched the Comanche as they came into this alien country. Senaqua, now pushing himself to become fully functional again, sent Mugual ahead, scouting. Both father and son seemed wary, watchful, and when they camped for the night Johnny asked for some reason.

Senaqua was silent for a moment. Then he said, "This is not the land we know. Our country is more open, and you can see an enemy long before he draws near, unless he has set up an ambush. This is like moving at night. You cannot see what may be hidden beyond the trees ahead or to the right or left. We Comanche have many enemies who will not realize that now we are white men.

"Most people of the forest country are somewhat peaceable, but even the Naconi and the Nacogdoche do not like our people, for we have been known to raid even here, into such strange country." He grunted a laugh. "When we come here, it is for stealing women or for making war. The tribes in the forest do not appreciate either endeavor."

Johnny stretched on his blanket, listening to the snap of the pine cones in the fire. "We haven't seen anyone since the Yankees, days and days ago," he said. "And we've been careful to camp far enough from the track so our fires can't be seen. The night should hide our smoke, too. I don't see that anyone could find us."

Senaqua, looking amused, had opened his mouth to speak when there came a shrill bird call through the night. He shook his head. "Mugual," he said, moving already to cover the fire with ashes and dirt.

The others melted into the darkness, and Johnny heard the quiet sound of horses being caught and pushed behind the wagon. The moon, still in its first quarter, gave little light and almost none came through the overhanging pine boughs to light the small clearing where they chose to camp.

Johnny, sliding into a tangle of bushes, felt someone near, and there was no mistaking the gamy smell of Senaqua. They waited in silence for Mugual to come.

But what came was the sound of hooves padding quietly on pine straw. Mugual had gone afoot, and Johnny tensed.

"I smell coffee," said a deep baritone. "I also smell smoke, not too far away. Someone is hiding here, waiting to find if I'm friend or foe, and I can tell you that while I may not be a friend, I am damn sure not an enemy. I haven't had a cup of coffee in weeks."

Johnny set his hand on Senaqua's shoulder. The Indian put his hand over Gannelli's and squeezed twice. Then the cultured British tones rose into the night.

"And who might you be, coming so late and alone?"

The hooves stopped. Johnny could imagine the man staring about, trying to find the speaker in the darkness. "Forrest Napier the Third, lately of New Orleans. You might call me a student of the laws of chance. One who is, at the moment, financially embarrassed."

"Wanted?" came the question in Ma's gruff voice from the other side of the clearing.

There was a quiet chuckle. "Who among us is entirely unwanted? By someone? Somewhere? I, however, find myself somewhat uncomfortably wanted by General Butler, who is at present rearranging the social scene in New Orleans." The tone held more than a touch of bitterness.

"He has made some most interesting rules of conduct for the citizens of that city. Any woman insulting any of his troops, or even, in some cases, refusing attentions from them, is treated as a harlot plying her trade. And the treatment given genuine harlots is beyond belief."

Hassie Mae struck a light, and the lantern bloomed into a yellow glow. Senaqua pushed dry pine cones into the coals amid the ash, and the fire began to rekindle. Ma Devinney brought the coffee pot, which had been in her hand when the alarm was given, and set it at the edge of the fire to heat again.

Mugual slid into the circle of light and stared across it at the newcomer, who was dismounting from his big bay gelding. Johnny stared, too.

Forrest Napier the Third was not really large enough to need such a big horse, standing a neat five-nine or so. He was dapper in a blue coat and tan trousers, but his boots were down-at-heel, though polished to a high gloss.

He looked exactly like what he claimed to be, a gambler down on his luck.

He also looked like one who refused to allow himself to become slovenly.

He pulled off the saddle and laid it on the ground beside the fire. Then he slapped his horse on the side. "Go graze, Bones, if you can find something green." The beast whickered and moved off toward the other bunch at the farther side of the clearing beyond the wagon.

Napier had the neat, closed features convenient for those in his trade. His bright blue eyes were lively, however, betraying his interest in the group about the fire.

Ma Devinney brought out another tin cup and poured coffee, padding the hot handle with folds of skirt. The smell of scorched serge filled the night, but Napier accepted the hot liquid with thanks.

He took a sip and sighed. "Just as good as I thought it would be," he said. "But what interests me is why such an ill-assorted bunch is sitting around in the middle of the woods, ninety miles from anyplace in particular."

Johnny, again sitting on his blanket, leaned back against his own saddle. "I take it that you're not a great advocate of our new military government," he said.

Napier glanced at him sharply. "Sounds like a leading question," he said. "And I ought to pussyfoot around it with great care, but I can hardly be wanted any more than I am already. I am supposed to be hanged or shot by any Union soldier who catches me. Wherefore I admit that I do not admire our conquerors at all."

"You'll find that we feel much the same," said Johnny. "What brought you to the attention of Butler?"

Napier held out his cup again, and Ma refilled it. Nursing the coffee cup between his hands, he looked about at the circle of faces, his gaze lingering longest on the two Comanche.

"It can't hurt to tell you," he began. "God knows, it isn't something I'm ashamed of, though some might think I should be. I had a girl I was fond of. She was no better than she should be, maybe, but she was warmhearted and I liked her a lot. She made her living off men, but that didn't bother me. In a way, I did, too."

Luke reached to poke a log-end into the fire, and Mugual set another chunk to burn. Napier watched, silent, until they were done. Then he took up the tale again.

"She was pretty and lively and spunky. Popular, too, but she was no fool. She'd lost two brothers in the War, and she hadn't any patience with Yankees of any stripe. Not even in a business way: she'd take a dollar from some poor crippled Reb and turn down five from a Yankee officer.

"That didn't go down well, and when Butler's decree was published, that finished her off. Three Union officers came into the place and spoke to her, and she turned them down cold. They killed her, right there, without another word spoken. Shot her through the head.

"I keep a revolver under the table, when I play, for insurance. I got all three while everybody yelled and milled around. Then I got out of there. Didn't even stop for my things up in my room, which is why I'm here instead of dangling from a rope."

Ma got up and moved to the wagon. She returned with the rest of the bacon and beans left from supper and set the skillet on the fire. She stirred the mess until it steamed, then offered it to Napier.

He glanced up, one eyebrow quirked. Then, realizing that this was acceptance of a sort, he took the skillet, set it on the ground, and dug in. He looked quite a bit less pale when he was finished and the last of the burnt-on crust was scraped off the sides of the pan.

"I take it that you have a project in hand," he said. "Something to make life interesting for our new friends in high places?"

Johnny glanced around the circle, and six heads nodded. "We intend to start a war of our own, no politics or economics involved. Just pure vengeance. We hope to make it pretty brisk, and we all have some abilities that should come in handy.

"We don't look terribly suspicious—at least I hope we don't—and we should be able to last for some time, once we go to work."

Napier stretched his feet to the fire and thrust his hands into his pockets. "Well, if a card sharp can help you at all, count me in. That would give me something to do. Earn my coffee, anyway."

Ma leaned forward to stare at him. "Eight is a good number, not too many or too few. I vote we take him on."

Hassie and Magda nodded.

"We'll all go together, a tiny army setting out to attack Goliath," said Johnny.

The two Comanche grunted, their black eyes bright in the firelight. Johnny grinned at Luke, and both turned to the new member of the group.

"Welcome to the Gannelli Family Circus," said Gian-Carlo Gannelli.

CHAPTER TWENTY

For days the newly formed group moved deeper into the forested hills. Day after day the hills got steeper, the trees bigger, and the clearings harder to find. They crossed creeks running bank-full with the frequent rains, and they sheltered from those same rains in groves of hickory or pine forests or stands of oak so thick-branched that very little of the moisture found its way down to them.

Though Luke had come through the region recently in company with Ma and Hassie Mae, he had been so withdrawn that he hadn't noticed much. Ma and Hassie were not the sort who knew enough about woods and creeks and trees to do much good, Johnny found.

Napier, however, had crossed the river at Shreve's Port and dropped southward to avoid the chance of meeting Union troops. He was a man who forgot little that he saw and nothing that he heard, and with his expert guidance Johnny managed to avoid most of the traveled roads. They kept to game trails and random tracks that seemed to lead no place in particular, sometimes having to hack a path for the wagon through the thick forest. Somehow they kept Johnny's army heading in the right direction.

Senaqua answered Gannelli's unvoiced question one morning while they jogged quietly along behind the wagon. "These are the ways taken by hunting and war parties. Once when I was very young I came this way with a raiding group after women and horses.

"We captured two white women from the Spaniards, as well as many horses. Some white-eyes came after us, and we fought all through the woods as we retreated with our booty. We lost only two men, while they lost at least a dozen, and we returned home with everything we had captured and weapons taken from their dead, as well." He grunted, as if remembering those lost days.

"It was my first raid and my last, for soon afterward I was captured and sold. But I remember trails like these. Possibly we came along this very route."

That startled Johnny. Senaqua was so quiet and gentlemanly that it was hard to keep in mind the fact that he had begun life as a savage, trained in all the pursuits that entailed. Even Mugual, perhaps because of his father, seemed quite civilized, when he wasn't being a typical boy.

In fact, Mugual was fascinated with learning to throw knives, as Johnny and Magda did. Every evening after supper, Magda took him aside and taught him the finer points of the art, and soon Johnny began taking part in those lessons. Mugual, fortunately, had a natural aptitude that made him learn quickly and well.

Once he felt he did that sufficiently skillfully, the boy began insisting upon being taught to ride the ponies standing up. That was not as easy as the knife-throwing, even though he was a marvelous horseman. For one thing, the ponies had been out of practice for a long time. They were also used to carrying packs, now, instead of trick riders. The music of Papa's fiddle and Mama's accordion had faded from their minds as well, and it took some doing to make them take up their old habits again. The rhythms of the music seemed an important element that was now lacking.

Camped one evening beneath a big hickory in a grassy glade, they were again giving riding lessons. Magda took Mugual into the edge of the forest for a bit of knife-play while Johnny tried to think of a way to get the ponies to take up the timing to which they must pace. There had to be a metronome-like quality if Mugual was to learn.

As he sat poking the fire, Forrest Napier dropped onto the group beside him. Supper was over, the tin pans and cups cleaned in the creek at the bottom of the slope. The skillet and coffeepot were ready for the morning meal, and he now seemed inclined to talk.

Johnny, caught up in his problem with the ponies, did not respond as usual, and the gambler asked, at last, "You are truly worried about teaching that young Indian to ride, aren't you? What's the problem?"

"Music. The little devils won't settle down and remember their routine until we have music to remind them. I sing like a crow and Magda is worse. Hassie hasn't a musical bone in her body, and I can't imagine what Ma's singing would be like. Mugual really does want to learn, and it might come in very handy for all of us if he does."

Napier reached into his waistcoat pocket. "If that is all you need, I can play my harmonica. What do the little beasts like to hear?"

Johnny felt a surge of laughter rise inside him. "*The Poet and Peasant Overture*," he managed to choke.

The ponies, grazing at the farther side of the glade, picked up their ears when the thin but familiar strains reached them. They turned to stare toward the fire, and Johnny whistled the double note call that summoned them to a performance. They came trotting together, their small hooves already picking up the tempo.

"Maggie! You and Mugual come quickly!" he called. "We have music, and the ponies are going to work!"

She and the boy bounced into the clearing as the ponies lined up side by side, tossing their manes and giving little snorts. Magda grinned and vaulted onto Pietro's back. Johnny leaped onto Bianca, and Napier struck up the overture again.

The little horses arched their necks and moved rhythmically around the fire as their riders stood easily on their backs. Johnny bent to place his hands on the back of Pietro, his feet still set on Bianca's sturdy haunches. Magda rose on one foot, her free leg sweeping into the arabesque her mother had taught her. Then both, at the same moment, flipped into double somersaults that ended with their feet planted solidly on the ground while the ponies kept on trotting.

The others had gathered to watch, and there came a spatter of applause. Then Mugual stepped into the circle and looked longingly at the ponies. That was the moment when his long and difficult labor began.

The boy was agile as a panther, very supple and strong, but he wanted to stand and ride at once, stepping effortlessly from one back to the other. So easy did the Gannellis make the trick look that he thought it would be simple.

He rode with the skill of his people, and he straddled Bianca, his long legs held up to keep his feet from dragging the ground. One leg he folded across before him, before setting the moccasined foot on the horse's back.

Cautiously, he went onto one knee and both hands, setting his feet at last together on the surging back. With a triumphant smile, he straightened, hands out to balance and tumbled headfirst to the ground. He took it hard, though his face went blank and his eyes were inscrutable.

Johnny gestured to the others to go about their business. There was no point in making the boy feel the humiliation of defeat before he had fairly begun. Then he and Magda mounted the ponies again, lifting Mugual between them. First with one, then with the other, they held him before them as he learned the rhythm, the flexing, the positions required for remaining upright and secure.

Once he found his balance, Mugual had little trouble riding in a standing position. He wore himself and the ponies down before Johnny called a halt.

"We must move in the morning, and the ponies need rest, if they are to carry loads. You are going to be stiff and sore, and you'll almost groan every time you move, Mugual. We will have many nights to work on this, and it simply cannot be done quickly and easily. You tell him, Senaqua."

Potesenaquahip was sitting beside the fire, laughing. For once, his Indian stoicism had deserted him, and he was almost rolling on the ground, his eyes moist with mirth. Wiping them on the back of his hand, he gasped for air as Johnny watched, puzzled.

"What is so funny about your son getting bounced on his head and bruised from top to toe?" he asked.

Pietro, standing nearby, waiting for the music to begin again, whiffled inquiringly, and Napier tapped his harmonica against his palm, removing the collected moisture before returning it to his pocket.

Ma slapped Bianca on the rump as she made her way to the wagon and her waiting blankets, and the ponies moved away at last, leaving Johnny to sit beside Senaqua as the Comanche regained control.

When he subsided at last, Senaqua sighed. "You probably think that I have gone mad," he said.

Johnny leaned against his saddle, placed by the fire to pillow his head for the night. "Not to say gone mad, but something is funny, and I can't see what that might be."

"In order to understand, you must know Mugual since he was an infant," the boy's father said. "I was older than most of my peers by the time I returned to my old way of life, and I married a childless woman whose man had been killed. It worked out rather better than most, and Mugual surprised us both by arriving after we believed that to be impossible. From his first day on earth, he seemed to be in control of everything about him."

Magda settled into her blankets on the other side of the fire and listened with interest. "Oh, surely a tiny baby has no control."

"Mugual did. He could wrap both of us about his finger, and he knew that from almost his first day. He was solemn and wise, and he never tried to cry. When he was born, his mother told me, he gave one deep gasp, but no other sound did he make."

Magda looked astonished. "I thought a baby had to be slapped to make it cry, when it is born. So it can breathe."

"That first cry is the only one allowed to a baby of my kind. Crying babies can mean death for their elders, in times of war and danger, so after it clears its lungs, we cover the nose and mouth. At that moment, it learns not to cry. But Mugual did not need even that. The old women of the tribe still talk about him with awe and wonder. He would lie on his furs, watching us, and when he wanted anything he would grunt like an old man. Of course his mother went at once, and I was not far behind.

"By the time he was big enough to learn to use his small bow and to ride, those things came easily to him. Other lads took tumbles, but not Mugual. When their rabbit traps caught only small birds, his caught rabbits."

Senaqua chuckled again. "When he tried to stand up on that pony and fell on his head, the expression on his face was just too much. It was completely shocked, as if the world had turned upside down. The boy expected to do as well as both of you, from the beginning. You made it look so easy."

"I still don't think that's funny," said Magda, and Johnny, knowing her tender heart, smiled at her. "He's only a boy, and you can't expect him to understand everything."

"But you do not understand," the Comanche said. "It is not that I feel nothing for his pain. He is the only child I will ever have, for his mother is dead and I have no intention of taking another wife. It is not *safe* to think that one controls his world. One has no caution until he learns danger, and without caution one cannot survive for long in this world. *N'est-ce pas?*"

Johnny nodded. He and his cousin had lived all their lives with danger. Falls from trapezes, from horses, from Papa's and Barnabas's broad shoulders that marked them from head to foot with bruises, when they were children, had taught them the perils of lost concentration. Such training fitted them very well, Gannelli realized, for the campaign they were about to begin.

"Do you think that Mugual will be reckless?" he asked Senaqua.

"He must learn that he does not move the sun across the sky or the wind through the trees. That will make him a safer companion," said his father. "But seeing him when he slid between the ponies, one foot still on the back of each that was a sight worth living a long time to see.

"If I seem heartless, it is not that. I feel for his bruises, even as I rejoice in them. They may save his life, one day. And ours."

So it was with even more care that the Gannellis ended every evening with a lesson in trick riding. Mugual learned with ridiculous ease, but never again did he show such reckless abandon as he had on that first night. He lost his remote expression and became more alert than before.

By the time they reached the creek that Senaqua called the Naconiche, his son was riding along with Johnny and Magda, trading ponies with growing ease. He had even learned to do handstands with some security, and he promised to become a credit to any circus.

His young face was battered, of course, and his feelings were probably scarred, as well, by blows to his ego.

But he kept his cheerful disposition, and Johnny was not sorry for taking the time to train him.

It was a fit and determined group that came near the old Spanish town of Nacogdoches, crossing the main north-south trail to bear east toward the Attoyac River. The forest was now of tremendous size, the trees huge in girth. The needles of the towering pines sang constantly in the wind overhead. It was perfect cover for a guerrilla army.

CHAPTER TWENTY-ONE

By late afternoon they had left behind the higher woodlands. In this lower, wetter country it was steamy hot, the canopy of leaves trapping the heat beneath their thick layers, as the sun seared down above. Johnny felt as if he had been dipped in oil and sautéed slowly.

He looked with longing toward the river's purling current as he helped to set up the camp on its bank. From this place, they would begin their small and self-contained war.

As the sun descended, the thickness of the hovering forest dimmed the light. The effect was almost stifling to those who had been used to the more open country.

Frogs tuned up down by the water, and tree toads began chirping shrilly in the branches above the camp. Every possible sort of night bird began calling to its fellows, and the entire chorus was counterpointed by the rhythmic hooting of owls.

Johnny could hear something that sounded like a cat fight, deep in the brush beyond the river. A bobcat family quarrel, Senaqua assured him. But beyond that, as twilight deepened, there came a long cry like a soul in dire distress.

Johnny knew that one, from his time in Arkansas. "Cougar."

Senaqua nodded. "You will find here almost every sort of animal and tree and bird that you ever heard of," he said. "The nights are not going to be silent, but we will be safe. We should, however, take thought for the horses. A cougar loves horsemeat almost as much as he loves the flesh of a human child."

Magda, passing with blankets piled in her arms, shuddered and grimaced at her cousin. "What a horrible thought!" she muttered.

He agreed, feeling a chill along his spine, despite the heat, as he stumbled with Napier through the dim forest, building a brush fence. This would pen the horses, temporarily, onto a grassy peninsula jutting out into the river.

They cut brush, tied it together with vines, tested it for strength all the way. By the time they finished, both were sweaty and weary, but the fence should hold any except a terrified horse inside its protection.

There was plenty of dead wood for their fire, though they kept only a small blaze, after their cooking was done, for its smoke would repel mosquitoes. From the sounds they heard in the forest, Johnny knew they must keep a flame also to hold away the beasts from which they wanted no visit.

At last he felt that he had thought of everything possible. He rose, stretched, and took up a blazing brand from the fire. "I am going down to the river to bathe and swim. It's dark and there are probably snakes, but if I remain in my clothes for another instant I am going to go mad. Does anyone want to go with me?" He glanced down at Luke and Napier.

Luke nodded. "Even if I have to wade through water moccasins," he said.

Napier had his coat off already. "Me, too, come what may."

The Comanche said nothing, but they were on their feet, ready to go, as well. Ma chuckled. "Go ahead, boys. We'll sit here and wait. Then when you have scared off the moccasins and the alligators, we women will go down there and bathe, too. I suspect that we're going to spend a right smart of time down there."

The water was almost blood-warm, and it smelled strange a mixture of greenery and mud and something indefinable yet rather sweet. Johnny had hoped the current would be cold, like the rivers in Arkansas, and he kept wading outward toward the middle of the stream. The bottom was uneven and muddy.

He felt a cooler current against his legs, just as he stepped off into a deep hole. His head went under, and he found that the water also tasted like mud.

He snorted to the surface to find his companions dim shapes thrust upward from the water. He paddled shoreward, where he scrubbed himself with handfuls of cattail leaves, removing the dirt and sweat. As he washed, he savored the coolness caused by evaporation. Almost he felt chilly.

Then he turned to swim out into the deeper water, but he paused, hearing a shout from the direction of the camp. Even as he headed for shore, there was the sound of a shot.

He scrambled up the bluff, followed by the other men, who grabbed their scanty clothing and struggled into it as they ran toward the fire. Before they came too near, the Comanche peeled off to right and left to circle the clearing.

The other three crept forward quietly, spreading to left and right of the game trail they had followed before. Johnny peered through a screen of huckleberry bushes toward the firelight. No one stood near the blaze, and the bulk of the wagon hid most of the clearing beyond it.

Johnny pushed through the bushes and moved forward, his knives, always present in his clothing, in his hands. Glancing about the firelit space, he saw motion at the farther edge. Someone was struggling on the ground.

He dashed forward and bent over a tangle of legs and skirts. Both Ma and Hassie were holding onto a skinny old man, who flopped about like a caught bass. As Johnny took hold of the man, both women rose, straightening their skirts and brushing away the clinging pine straw and dirt.

"Where is Maggie?" asked Johnny, his voice tense.

Ma pointed off into the woods. "She run off after the other one. They sneaked in and almost stole a sack of supplies before we knowed they was here at all."

Hassie was panting, her forehead marked with a streak of blood along a scratch. "These are a couple of slick ones," she gasped. "I was looking right at them and didn't see anything for a long time. Then when I finally realized what was there I yelled, and Ma jumped this one. The other took off into the woods with Maggie right after him or her."

Mugual had gone in the direction taken by the fugitive. Even if Maggie caught up to him, the boy would be close by, which was reassuring. There wasn't anyone he knew who could match the boy's fleetness of foot.

He pulled the man into the firelight and turned him about to examine him. The wizened face jerked from side to side as if looking for a way to escape, but now he was surrounded by his captors.

"He ain't an Injun," said Ma, glancing at Senaqua.

"No. Unless there are more gray-eyed Indians than I know about," said the Comanche.

Johnny stared into the dirty face and saw that the eyes, almost buried in the folds of wrinkled eyelids, were the color of slate. The old man was ragged, almost naked; his skin was the shade of leaf mold on the floor of the forest, whether naturally or because of accumulated grime Johnny could not determine. Though the captive looked frail, Johnny knew that Ma and Hassie Mae were no weaklings, so he had to be stronger than he seemed.

There came a sound from the forest, whimpers and muffled shrieks. Napier moved into the wood, toward the noise, and in a moment he emerged again, followed by

Magda. The complicated shape behind her resolved itself into Mugual and a prisoner, held tightly from behind. The bare feet kicked and flapped at the ground, for the boy was carrying the captive.

"I caught her, but it wasn't easy," Magda panted. "I never could have held her if Mugual hadn't come. She is a wildcat!"

Johnny had to take his cousin's word; he never would have thought the creature Mugual set down before the fire was female. It could have been anything, not necessarily of the human kind. Though the man had not uttered a sound, this one carried on a constant moaning, punctuated by occasional eerie shrieks. She dashed to the man and crouched on the ground by his feet, holding onto his knees. He, however, did not look down but kept his narrowed eyes focused on his captors.

Johnny sighed. It was up to him to find out who these wild people might be. "Do you speak English?" he asked.

The gray eyes turned toward him. The wrinkled face grimaced, and the old fellow spat at his feet. *"¡Inglés!"* he snarled. *"Sí, un poco."* He surveyed Johnny with hostility. *"¡Hijo de puta!"*

Magda giggled. "You do not want to know what he called you," she told Johnny. "But he evidently does speak a bit of English, and I certainly don't recall enough Spanish to question him intelligently.

Johnny gazed into those opaque eyes. "Who are you? Why are you here in the forest?"

The old man shuddered convulsively. He drew himself up to his full height, which was surprising once the curve of his back went straight. His head was finely shaped, and there was something of the hawk in the shape of nose and jaw.

"I am...Jorge Vásquez de García. This..."—he gestured contemptuously at the figure at his feet—"...was my child, when she was not *demente*. We are here for that Anglos drove us from our home, our land. We live like beasts, for no one have a charity for us. We find another spot, build house, but they drove us from that as well. Anglos, they take all for their own. We try to build no more, but hide in the forest. The wild creature, he have more mercy for us than the Anglos."

The woman sobbed, hugging his knees harder. He looked down and shook his head. "She was weak, and now she is nothing. But we live still." He stared proudly into Johnny's face, and behind the filthy skin and the tangle of hair Johnny could see the ghost of a Spanish grandee, lost amid years and hardships.

In the faces of his companions Johnny saw an echo of his own anger. These people, too, had suffered at the hands of others. Their story was not unlike that of the rest of them, but it had lasted far longer, that was evident.

Ma Devinney stepped forward and tugged at the woman's arm. She had, in some way, found a cup of coffee in the confusion and now she held it out to the battered girl. "Here, child, you drink this. You'll feel better. Then you can go down to the river with the girls and me, and we'll get some of the dirt off you."

Johnny glanced from face to face. There was no need for words, he could see, for these were outcasts of their own stamp. Not a hint of dissent could he see as the girl looked up to see something in the old woman's face that reassured her.

She held out a grubby hand for the cup. When the hot liquid warmed her from inside out, she relaxed her hold on her father's legs with her free arm and struggled to her feet. The shivering that had shaken her eased.

"¿Hija?" Her father was staring at her. "¿Cómo está?"

She did not reply, though she looked into his face without cringing. That seemed to Johnny to be a hopeful sign.

Luke touched his arm. "I think we might back off. Let them catch their breath and find out they can trust us. That girl hasn't anything wrong with her except being frightened out of her wits for so long."

Johnny turned toward him, and Luke grimaced. "One of the children I lost was a girl. Fourteen. I know girls, and this poor creature is not much more than that. She isn't nearly as old as she looks. You watch. I know what I am talking about."

They moved away together, leaving the three women near the wagon. Although he didn't make it obvious, Johnny remained near enough to watch the two Spaniards. But when the women led the girl toward the river, he began to relax.

At last he spread his blanket far enough from the fire to avoid the heat, but near enough to toss fresh wood onto the coals. Big cats fear fire, and he did not intend to risk a visit from a bobcat or cougar.

The old man stood beside the wagon, but after his daughter left, he stirred and turned toward the spot where Johnny was reclining on his blanket. He paused some distance from him, as if wondering about his welcome.

"You and your people you want us to stay? Here?" He sounded as if he could not believe that.

Johnny gestured for him to sit. He dribbled the last of the coffee from the pot and handed the cup to the old man. "*Señor*, we, too, are outcasts. We are wanted by the law of this new government, and we are here to make war on their troops that move into this country. I suspect that you know the river bottoms as nobody else can. You might be interested in helping us, for you have your own score to settle.

"Your knowledge of the river and the swamps and the forest can be valuable to us, for we intend to hit and run. If we know where to hide, how to go where troops cannot follow us, it will be a good thing. Do you understand?"

Jorge Vásquez de García began to smile. His face almost cracked with the unaccustomed exercise, and he held out his hand.

It felt claw-like in Johnny's, dry and hard and rough. But it was strong with the awesome strength of one who is determined to survive.

As they grasped hands, the three women returned from the river, leading the girl they had taken with them. Johnny stared, and García started. He moved toward his daughter, incredulity in his expression.

"¿Manuela? ¿Es tú?"

Johnny understood. A ragged, filthy hag had gone down the path. The woman returning was scrubbed clean, her hair washed and combed roughly. She wore a dress of Hassie Mae's, too large but becoming on her slender, tough figure.

Her face was smooth and oval, and its tan did not detract from its loveliness. As her hair dried, it gleamed black and lustrous.

Johnny caught Magda's eye, and his cousin grinned impishly. He grinned back. Their new recruits were surprising ones, if nothing else. Perhaps they would be far more valuable than they had seemed, at first, capable of becoming.

CHAPTER TWENTY-TWO

Johnny found life there in the Big Thicket far different even from that in the wooded mountains of Arkansas or the wooded Delta of Mississippi. But those had been older, more settled places. This heavy forest stretched from the Gulf of Mexico northward, and its riverbanks were as wild as anything Johnny would have expected to find in Africa.

They took some time to settle in before beginning their campaign. They had to create a secure base of operations, along with alternates in case of hot pursuit. They needed more horses and supplies, as well as respectable clothing that would let Hassie or Ma go into Nacogdoches to shop. As Johnny had no intention of adding robbery to his crimes, he knew they would have to use their scanty supply of money with caution. The habit of Yankee-hunting was, he found, going to be expensive.

They chose to build their permanent camp deep in the woods, farther from the river than that first camp had been. It was watered by a creek fed by a spring that headed in deep sand.

They constructed a rough log house that would keep the winter wind and rain off them and their supplies, roofing it tightly with branches, leaves, and slabs axed from the logs they felled. For the horses they built pens of poles reinforced with brush, well removed from the cabin and yet within hearing distance.

This took advantage of a natural clearing, the result of some forest fire of past years. It was studded with young pines and hardwoods, yet waist deep with lush grass.

Weary and yet filled with satisfaction, Johnny felt that nobody in the world knew of the existence of his troop. By all logic, the Union Captain should believe that he and Magda were headed west, as so many other outlaws had gone. Mugual and Seneca were simply Indians, indistinguishable from any others of their kind to the unknowing eye.

Napier was well away from the scene of his crime, and Luke was of no concern to anyone. Ma and Hassie Mae were the picture of respectability. No, this unlikely group of revolutionaries should not be the object of anyone's search.

Once the camp was finished to everyone's satisfaction, Johnny called a strategy meeting. "It's time to begin thinking about what we intend to do. I don't want to rob anyone; preying on any neighbors we might have just doesn't make sense," he began. "The people around here aren't going to be overly fond of the occupying troops, that is certain, and they may even help us, once they find out what we are trying to accomplish. So we won't bother anybody. Are there any suggestions? And does anybody have any money?"

Ma Devinney sighed deeply and turned back her serge skirt, together with numbers of petticoats. She extended her sturdy right leg, which was clad in a kittenish pantalette finished off with lace insertion tied with blue bows.

She untied the top bow and ran her fingers behind her knee. When they emerged from the billow of cloth, they held a cloth bag.

"I figured this might come in handy, whatever came. We'll see how far this will go," she said.

Senaqua, sitting closest to her, poured the contents of the bag into his broad palm. The unmistakable ring of gold on gold filled the air with its delicate tinkle.

The Comanche's dark eyes widened fractionally. "Three double eagles," he said. He piled them on the blanket on which he sat. "One, two, three. A dozen half eagles, very worn but passable."

Johnny had sat up straight, his gaze fixed on the growing pile of gold coins. But Senaqua was not finished.

"Let me count, here. Fifteen Liberty dollars. A fortune, Madame, in these cashless times. A hundred and thirty-five dollars in all. It should be enough to help greatly, if we use it wisely."

A sigh ran around the fire. Johnny smiled. "That is a good beginning. Magda and I have a handful of silver we retrieved from the Gannelli circus. Perhaps we can supply ourselves sufficiently with this. And in time we may arm ourselves by looting our victims."

Forrest Napier laughed. "If you can't, I can fill in some gaps."

Ma turned and stared. "I thought you was too broke when you come up to us even to buy coffee!"

He chuckled. "Not too broke—too cautious to go where coffee could be purchased. But I took the liberty of relieving my military victims of their cash before I fled the scene of carnage. They had no more use for it, and I took it without a qualm.

"But spending it was another matter. I would have been recognized because of the excellent likeness on the wanted posters Butler circulated. Here!" He pulled a thin wallet from an inner pocket and laid it in Johnny's hand.

Inside was three hundred dollars in Yankee paper money. To that, Napier added a handful of small gold coins from his pack.

"Well, we seem to be in business," said Johnny. "Ma, could you and Hassie Mae go into San Augustine tomorrow, and see what you can pick up without using so much cash that somebody will get suspicious?"

Ma grinned. "You think you're going to have to twist my arm to get me to go shopping?" she asked.

* * * * * * *

The next morning they polished up Ma's wagon and hitched to it the worn-out horse that had pulled it all the way from Alatosa. After days of rest and a bellyful of good grass, he looked much better, and even tried to kick at the shafts.

The two women brushed their serge garments and washed and smoothed their linen. Hair brushed and faces shining, they looked poor but self-respecting—just right for their errand. In her threadbare reticule Ma carried all the copper and small silver money, with a few of the smaller gold coins.

"I'll pick up enough material to make a rich-widow dress," said Ma. "Then when we look as if we should legitimately have money, we'll go back and get the expensive things. For now we'll just pick up meal and coffee and harness mending materials. Is there anything else we need bad?"

Johnny glanced about, but every head shook. Satisfied, Ma clucked to the horse, and they made off down the narrow, twisting track they had cut through the forest for the passage of the wagon. As she went through, they filled the space with brush, so that no chance hunter would notice the trace. Mugual swept behind the tall wheels with a broken branch, removing the tracks all the way to Camino Real, the main road eastward.

It was a long way to San Augustine some twelve or fifteen miles. The small Anglo community on Ayish Bayou was at least a day and a half away, allowing for getting over the fords, resting the horse, and following the sinuous route through the endless forest. It would be four days, at least, before Ma returned, and possibly, given the bad luck of a broken wheel or such, even more.

Once the wagon was out of sight, Johnny found work for all hands. Otherwise he knew that they would worry hard all the while.

Set hooks lined the willow-grown banks of the river and the edges of the sloughs and the eddy pools. Mugual and Senaqua tended those, ordinarily, but now Mugual had to follow the wagon to its junction with the main road, so Napier went with the Comanche to run the lines.

Magda was rummaging through the wood, having set herself to find every edible plant it would afford them. As Manuela had been living on wild foods for years, she went with her to give her lessons in what was safe to eat and what was not. The two disappeared into the trees and their voices died away into the distance.

That left Johnny in the clearing before the door of their house. Luke and the Spaniard stood there, and Luke was staring at a stump loaded with battered harness. "I'd better make myself useful, or Ma will have my skin when she gets back," he said. He moved on his crutch over to their small supply of spare leather.

Jorge Vásquez de García looked at Johnny. "I will teach you the best ways through the forest. If you want, I shall begin now, while we wait. You will worry, I know that well. But if we are busy, you will have no time. We go?"

Johnny nodded. "Good thinking. I need to know how to find my way around. We all do, and you can take turns with us, when there is time. We should be able to find our way back here blindfold or full of lead. We needn't think the Yankees will oblige us by doing all their searching for us by daylight."

The skinny shape moved toward the wall of green. "Come," he said.

Johnny had never thought that trees might be as individual as people. He had used game trails for all his life, without being truly conscious of their individuality and that of the growths about them.

Now Jorge showed him the distinctive gnarls and patterns of branches, the lumps and colors and twists that made every tree different from others like it. And, of course, he pointed out the useful ones, the hickory and the pecan with their rich nuts, the sweetgum and the ash and the elm. A dozen kinds of oaks grew there, and every trail they followed or crossed was festooned with vines.

As they crossed one such narrow track, Jorge touched Johnny's shoulder. "What is that there in the dust?" he asked, pointing downward.

Johnny studied the big prints, large as his own hand with fingers outspread. At one edge there were tiny prick-marks.

"Here is like cat track, the cougar. Here is bear. Big sow. Behind come others. You see?—a cub."

Luke had said there were black bear in this country. Johnny had seen a few as the circus traveled the wooded roads of the south, but the thought was unsettling. Bears sometimes attacked horses.

"We need a dog," he muttered, half to himself.

"*¿Qué dice?*"

"A dog." Johnny thought for a moment. "*Un perro.* To let us know if anything bothers the horses. It would be useful to have one with the mounts and another at the house, in fact. Two dogs."

Jorge straightened his skinny back and stared into the trees. "One has dogs. Well-trained *animales*. He is black—does that trouble you?"

"I wasn't a Reb," Johnny protested. "Nor yet a Yankee. My people, we were artistes, and we pay no attention to such matters. A black man can applaud as loudly as a white one. We met many on our travels who helped us. No, that doesn't bother me. Was he a slave?"

"Once, long past. He go into Thicket, which is a place made for runaways. There is so much, and all is difficult to travel." Jorge's face was solemn, and Johnny knew he thought of his own long years of exile.

Then he brightened. "I take you there. Three hours, no more. When we return to camp, it will be late, no time to worry. We will have dogs—fine dogs, who understand what we say. Come."

Once again they moved through the soaring trees, the tangled vines and bushes. Sometimes taking advantage of game trails, sometimes pushing through the light under-growth, Jorge seemed to have a built-in compass, for he never faltered. When the sun was almost overhead, they emerged from thick woods into a clearing.

At the farther side, almost hidden in thick vines, was a sort of shelter. It blended so well into the bushes and vines that if he had not known to look for it, Johnny would never have spotted it at all.

"Here," said Jorge, "is the house of Absalom. And here we find dogs."

He could have saved his breath, for as they stepped out of the trees a terrific din began beyond the weathered hut. At least dozens of dogs seemed to be letting their owner know that he had company.

CHAPTER TWENTY-THREE

Jorge paused near the edge of the clearing amid a din of bays and yelps and hoarse barks. "Absalom!" he shouted. "Is García! A friend comes, and there is no danger."

They waited, letting the man they wanted take his time in deciding whether or not to reply. At last there was a faint rustle amid the tangle of leaves off to their right, and a dark face came into view. It was followed by a lanky body clad in the tatters of faded blue overalls.

"Who be that with you?" Absalom asked. "Don't look like nobody I knows from around here."

"I'm not from around here," said Johnny, extending a hand. "I am happy to meet you, Mr. Absalom."

The term Mr. as applied to himself apparently stunned the black man for a few moments. He stood, eyes veiled, examining this newcomer into his domain.

His face was as thin as his body, lined with age, and marked with scars that latticed its right side. The lip there was curled into a permanent half smile by the long mark cutting right down his cheek. That lash mark gave him a quizzical expression that was belied by his cold and assessing eyes.

"You one of them that come with a bunch of folks upriver. Made camp, then moved off into the woods and built a cabin. Got horses and a wagon. I seen you when you come. I keeps an eye on anybody comes down here. You runnin'?" he asked.

Mugual had been on watch, and nothing much escaped his expert attention as he ranged about camp, eyes peeled for anything out of the ordinary. If Absalom had watched from cover without being detected by the Comanche it spoke highly of his abilities. Even Potesenaquahip hadn't sensed his watchful gaze, and that Indian was sensitive even to the presence of animals.

"Not exactly on the run," he said, choosing his words carefully. "We are going to...."—he made a lightning swift decision, shrugged, and went forward—"...We intend to make war on the Yankee troops that will be stationed in this area. You may not want to help us, though. They got your people freed."

"Didn't free me. When Ole Marse was whupping me with his bullwhip, didn't no Yankee come to make him stop. Onliest one that freed Absalom was Absalom." He cocked his head.

"You goin' to need a heap of luck and eyes in the backs of your heads, if you intends to tackle them Yankees. They got lots of men, over to San Augustine and cross the river in Nacogdoches. Anything I kin do, I will. I don't like nobody but folks what hides out in the swamps."

Jorge had been listening with a tight smile on his thin lips. "We need dogs," he said. "Two. Big, wise, understanding of human speech. Have you such to spare?"

Absalom turned and whistled twice, two descending notes. A big black dog came around the corner of the hut and stood regarding him questioningly.

Three short whistles, followed by a long trill, brought forth a slightly smaller animal, reddish with a black belly and legs. She came out of the woods and stood quietly beside her master, waiting for instructions.

"They didn't bark," Johnny said. "We need a watch-dog that will let us know when something gets too close to camp."

Absalom chuckled. "How you think I knowed to hide in the brush? These two don't raise Cain like the young'uns back in the pen. They comes to me and tells me that something's up. They asks me what they ought to do about it, and I tells 'em, and they does it."

"I wouldn't want to take your only real protection," said Johnny. "But they certainly do look intelligent."

"Don't worry. I'd never give up my last two trained dogs," the black said. "But these is just two. I got plenty more, all around you and hid in the brush. If you looked like you might hurt me, they'd be all over you. But you kin have Sue and Midnight. They likes folks, once I've introduced 'em."

"And what do you want for them? We have a bit of money, if that would help out."

"Where would I spend money?" Absalom laughed. "I can't go to town. Everybody round here knows me, and free or not free, I ain't goin' to risk bein' took back to Old Marse. He don't pay no never mind to Yankees or laws or nothin' else. I has stood for my last whupping.

"No, you just keep an eye out for me, like as I intends to do for you. If I needs something, maybe you can help me out. Like George and me has done for years now." He glanced about, his expression curious. "Where's your girl, George? You ain't lost her?"

Jorge shook his head. "She is with Juanito's people. There is young woman, *un poco* younger than Manuela, and they have become *amigos*. I could wish nothing better for *mi pobre niño*. I had thought that her mind had turned, but it was not, *gracias a Dios!*"

Absalom nodded, kneeling in the dusty grass of the clearing, and clicked his fingers sharply. Both dogs came to sit beside him, and Johnny obeyed his nod and approached as well.

"Here, Midnight," said Absalom, putting his hand on the head of the black.

Its dark gaze regarded Johnny curiously as it waited for instruction. Absalom put the other hand onto the back of the bitch, and she also turned her eyes toward this new master. Both sat patiently, tongues lolling.

"You goin' with these folks, you hear me? You knows George from away back. Now this here is Johnny. He's going to be your boss from now on. He'll tell you what to do, and I want you should listen hard and do just like he say. You hear me?"

He said this twice, once to each dog. When he was done, both rose in a dignified manner and went to sniff at Johnny's legs and his extended hand. Then, after searching glances at his face, both lay down beside his boots.

"You in fine shape now," said Absalom. "They'll do what you tells 'em and make friends with whoever you say." He rose stiffly from his knees and looked proudly at his former watchdogs.

Johnny, impressed, smiled at the man. "This is a wonderful gift, my friend. If you need anything, just let us know. And if we bring down more company after us than you like, we will warn you so you can hide yourself and your animals. If you are as invisible as they are, it will be impossible to find you."

The black laughed. "I hides even better than the dogs does," he said. "They ain't never been whupped or mistreated, so they don't have the need like I has. Besides, I don't rightly like company much at all any more."

With that, he turned and slipped into the brush again. The leaves barely stirred, and he was gone as if he had never existed.

Johnny imitated the snap of the fingers used by their master, and both sets of ears flipped upright instantly. The dogs rose and stood ready to move at his signal.

"Let's go, Midnight," he said. "Ready to go, Sue. Come on, now."

He moved back along the faint track by which they had approached the clearing. Jorge fell in behind him, while Midnight ranged ahead and Sue brought up the rear. As soon as they were in the forest, both dogs moved away from the path, keeping within sight but slipping almost noiselessly through the undergrowth.

A rabbit broke from a thicket and crossed almost under Midnight's nose. The dog didn't spare a glance for it, and Sue likewise ignored it.

Johnny halted in his tracks. "I never saw a dog that wouldn't chase a rabbit!" he said. "Are you sure these animals will do the job we need done?"

Jorge chuckled. "These are not hunting dogs. Absalom does not want his beasts to forget their tasks for a moment. He feeds them well, from his own hand, and he punished them severely when they were small for chasing birds and small game. These two will not look aside from their work for anything.

"Believe me, *amigo*, these are the very animals that we need. But we must feed them, and that will require a bit more hunting to keep them supplied. Count them as new *soldados* for our cause, no? They understand as well as most men, you will see."

By late afternoon they reached their own hidden hut. Midnight and Sue brought attention from those waiting there for the return of the two men, and Johnny introduced each of his companions, one by one, to the dogs. Once the pair had scanned and sniffed Luke and Napier, Manuela and Magda, they seemed to accept them fully.

Johnny knew with sudden certainty that, by day or night, the watchdogs would know every one of his people infallibly. It was a comfort to have them ranging through the night-bound forest, once the wood grew dark. He had an intuition that even a cougar or a bear would think twice before tackling his new recruits.

CHAPTER TWENTY-FOUR

It had been a long time since Johnny had known just what day it was. Now, as he waited for Ma and Hassie Mae to return from San Augustine, he found himself wondering if they had left on Tuesday or Wednesday or even Thursday. Luke and Napier passed their spare time in arguing the point, but Johnny didn't join in their good humored bickering. He worried quietly, no matter how busy he kept himself, and at last he was all but ready to send out Mugual to meet the wagon.

Senaqua, however, discouraged that. "It is hot, but it is still wet from the heavy rains. The roads are rotten, still, and the mud very deep. They will have to travel very slowly, and they may have encountered problems we did not foresee. Wait until tomorrow afternoon, at the least. Then send the boy, if you must," he said.

So Johnny waited. He fished, cut wood for the cook fire, hunted with the dogs through the forest after any trace of man. But time passed very slowly, nevertheless, and he saw the sun slip down the west beyond the thick layer of tree branches with much relief on that last day. There being no sign of the wagon, he nodded to Mugual. The boy set out at once.

The sun went down, and they ate supper listening through the clamor of frogs and crickets and whippoorwills for the sound of the horse's hooves, the creaks and clinks of the wagon. No alien sound, however, could be heard in the woods about them.

Well after dark, Mugual slipped into the circle of fire-light to join his father, who sat on his blanket, eyes closed, waiting stoically. The rest of the group left their evening conversations to ask questions, but the boy had no answers.

"No come," he said. His black eyes glinted in the fire-light as he shook his head. "Wait long. Wagon come—not right one. Long after night, I still wait, but they no come, so I am back."

The fire hissed as Manuela damped the blaze, making thick smoke to discourage the voracious mosquitoes that sang in their ears and tasted their blood. Magda crossed the clearing after dumping the dishwater, wiping her hands on her pants and looking tired and sweaty.

They sat in the damp heat of the night, keeping close to the smudge of smoke, though it all but stifled them. At last Johnny yawned. "We should go to bed," he said. "Sitting here and worrying won't bring them one minute sooner."

Long after he lay on his folded blanket, cursing the prickly wool that held heat against his body, Johnny could see the dark shapes of the Comanche still sitting by the dead fire. They seldom talked between themselves, and yet they always seemed to know each other's minds, without words.

With the dogs now on guard, with nobody knowing they were in the woods at all, they had not set a watch. From time to time one of the cool noses would touch Johnny's hand, and he would mutter encouragement to the tireless canine sentries. But in time he fell asleep, steaming in his own sweat. He turned often and dreamed ill dreams.

Suddenly, deep in the night, he woke and lay listening. A sound that wasn't part of the natural nightly clamor had come to his ears even in his sleep. He rose silently and went to the fire, where the Comanche had waited, but neither was there.

If there had been danger, Senaqua would have waked him, or the dogs would have come to nose him out of sleep. What else might have taken the Indians off into the night? Troubled, Johnny moved to the center of the clearing and looked up at the stars.

Orion was out of sight behind the trees. The fragment of moon was long gone. It must be well past midnight, probably only a couple of hours before dawn.

He kicked the ashes until the found the glow of coals. Then he laid pine straw and cones on the red glimmers until a blaze licked upward. When the fire was going well, he set the coffee pot in the edge of the coals to heat, for he knew he would not sleep again.

The sound of a whinny came to his ears now. That must have been what waked him, too far off to bring him awake: Ma's horse. He began to grin.

Magda came out of the house, which she shared by night with the other women, rubbing her eyes and yawning. "Did I hear a horse?" she asked.

"You did. Old Turk was calling to his friends, I think. And Senaqua and Mugual must have gone to meet them and clear the trail ahead of the wagon. Do you want to go with me or wait here?"

She wiped her eyes on the back of a wrist. "I need to wash up and dress. I'll start breakfast so it'll be done by the time you get back." He looked up through the branches at a mockingbird, singing its pre-dawn carol with unseemly vigor for so early in the morning.

"It's a wonder we could hear the horse over the braying of that devil," his cousin grumbled.

Johnny went chuckling up the brush-tangled trail. Magda did like to sleep!

After some time he saw a light bobbing along through the dark wood, blinking as tree trunks came between his position and that of the wagon.

He whistled, the long skree of a hawk that Senaqua had taught him to use. No hawk in his right mind would be flying through the woods at night, but that was far better, if overheard by enemy ears, than a yell would be.

A precise *"whippoorwill!"* came back from the distance. He knew it must be Mugual's call, though it could not have sounded more natural. That boy could mimic any bird or beast he ever heard.

Johnny sped along as well as he could, avoiding saw-vines and deadfall. Soon he saw the lantern swinging from the metal hook on the front of the wagon. Then he saw the wagon itself, but it wasn't the one he knew. It didn't creak and rattle and groan as that had done.

This was a trap, not a wagon at all. The old horse moved far more quickly and easily than he had done pulling the heavier vehicle.

"Ma?" he called, not loud but the word echoed through the trees and the birds paused for a moment in their early morning calling.

"Boy, you come here and see what we've got. You are going to drop your teeth!" Her raspy voice was the most welcome sound he had heard in days.

The light seemed impossibly bright as he neared the vehicle. The high wheels were obviously better able to cope with deep ruts and fords than those of the wagon had been. The trap itself was or had recently been polished to a high gloss, and gleams of black paint still shone through splashes of mud when the lantern swung.

"How about this for a perfect rich-widow rig, Johnny?" asked Hassie Mae. "And you should see the material we got! Some crazy Yankee has already come down to set up shop in San Augustine. Never seemed to understand that nobody down here was going to have any money except Confederate, and that wasn't going to be worth more'n so much tin.

"He's already put his prices so low he has to be taking a loss, just to move his stock. When he saw real silver coins, he almost cried, he was so happy. We never even had to hint we might have gold."

Now they moved through the wood even more quickly, for the Comanche were, indeed, removing the debris that camouflaged the track. Johnny added his own efforts to theirs, making it go even faster.

They assured Johnny that when morning dawned, one of them would go to the junction of track with road and brush out any trace of a turnoff. With that off his mind, Gannelli found himself, sooner than he would have thought, back at camp.

He smelled coffee and beans long before he arrived. The rest of the group had already risen and dressed, and the two girls had the last of the bacon sputtering in the long-handled frying pan.

Ma climbed down off the high seat of the rig with a sigh of relief. Only then did Johnny see that she held her left arm stiffly, as if it pained her.

Hassie crawled down, to stand hanging onto the braces. Her right foot was held off the ground, and Johnny now saw that there was blood on her boot.

He helped the women to the fire, where they sat on blocks of wood. "What happened?" he asked, examining Ma's arm, which was not broken but bruised. "Were you attacked?"

"Might say that," said Ma. "There's a dead man in the back of the rig. Tried to stop us, would you believe that? What's worse, he's the nephew of the sheriff over there. We'd better do our shopping in Nacogdoches, far as it is, from now on."

Johnny moved to the back of the trap and pulled aside the tarpaulin covering the supplies. Blank gray eyes stared up at him from a face whose sunburn was only a dark stain over the ashen hue of death.

"Tell us what happened," he said to Ma. "We'll bury him when its daylight."

She sighed again. "This specimen took a fancy to Hassie Mae. You know that girl is no flirt, and we were busy finding what we needed and keeping a low profile, but he kept getting in our way and making a real nuisance of himself.

"Hassie complained to Mr. Daland about that, and he run the scamp out of his store, but you could see he was scared to do it. Told us as soon as he was gone that we'd better watch our step, the sheriff being a mite foolish about his kin." She accepted a cup of coffee from Magda, blew on the hot liquid, and drank deeply.

"We didn't take much notice of that; we'd found an old couple who had this trap, and they needed a wagon to get their crop to town from their farm. The local Reb troop commandeered all the wagons when they went off to fight the Yankees, and nobody had much left to build another one with.

"They wanted our wagon, and we decided that the rig was just what we need to finish up our disguise." She paused for breath and took another long draught of coffee.

Hassie took up the tale. "We had to wait for the deal to be finished, so we spent the night in the wagon. That idiot came sniffing around in the night, and Ma ran him off with her shotgun. We thought that would end it for good." She frowned down at the tin cup in her own hands.

By then the group had settled to bacon and beans and coffee. Ma, declining the food, had her breath back. "We made the swap nice and early, finished up our shopping, and hitched old Turk up to the new outfit.

"We started for home, never thinking that we'd have trouble from anybody. There are a lot of people moving across country these days, and nobody seemed to be surprised to see strangers in town.

"There's a long hill just this side of town where the woods are mighty thick and the road is so muddy you have to keep your eye on your driving. While we were worrying our way through the loblolly other wagons had made there, this idiot came tearing up after us, whooping and shooting.

"It was pure D. luck that nobody else was on the road and there wasn't any house or farm in sight. When he lassoed Hassie and drug her out of the trap, I upped with the shotgun and stopped him. Didn't have time to aim right, and the thing dang near broke my arm."

Luke went back to the trap and uncovered the dead man. "You sure as hell stopped him," he said. "I never saw a hole any larger than that one."

"Will anybody come looking?" asked Johnny. "That could make a problem."

Hassie snorted. "He'd been sniffing around every skirt in town for years. Went from one to the other like a drunk bumblebee, the storekeeper told us. We cleaned the blood off his saddle and swatted his horse to make it go home. If anybody figures real hard, they probably will think he got thrown."

"All we have to do is bury him," said Ma. She glanced toward the trap and shuddered.

There was room in the forest to bury an army. Johnny and Forrest did the honors, while Senaqua and Mugual went back to erase all signs that the trap had turned into or gone through the wood. When they all met again in the clearing at the house, the dogs came, at last, to meet the newcomers.

Ma took one look and tore out for the house, holding her serge skirts high. "'Fore God!" she yelled. "Where did those monsters come from?"

Magda called the animals to heel while Johnny caught and calmed Ma. "They're ours," he said. "Jorge has a friend who raises dogs back in the woods. They'll keep varmints off the stock and out of the yard too. Hold on and calm down. What's the problem with them, anyway?"

"Never saw a dog in my life that didn't think I was something to eat," she said. She stepped into the door of the cabin and closed it behind her. "Don't bark much, do they?" she asked through the solid panel.

Johnny opened the door and pulled her out, protesting. "Come, Midnight, come Sue!" he said.

The dogs came forward until their noses were level with Johnny's knees. Both looked up inquiringly.

"This is Ma. She's a friend. You mind her, do you understand?"

Midnight stepped forward one pace and waited for Ma to make the first move. Still dubious, she offered the back of her hand for the dog to sniff.

"Good dog," she quavered.

By the time Sue had acknowledged her new acquaintance, Ma seemed reassured. "Right like people, ain't they?" she asked. "Real polite and quiet. Never thought I'd be able to get along with a dog, but these—you sure they won't forget who I am?"

Jorge came forward and took her worn hand. "*Señora*, I give you my word. The dogs of Absalom, my friend, are trustworthy. They will be good allies for all of us in the time to come."

Ma began to smile. "A good thing, too. There's going to be a big batch of Yankee cavalry and infantry coming in soon. They pulled 'em out of someplace west of here, and they'll be in Nacogdoches, mainly. But their big job will be keeping order all over this part of the country. I heard talk in San Augustine about that."

Johnny straightened, taking a deep breath and feeling excitement rise inside him. His war, long awaited and anticipated, was about to begin.

CHAPTER TWENTY-FIVE

It was Jorge who showed Johnny and his troop the best spots from which to watch travelers along the Camino. He knew the perfect place in which to set an ambush and the most obscure routes along which to make an escape. Amid the tangles of berry vines, haw, huckleberry, and button-bush along the low routes he took, even seasoned campaigners would lose their quarry.

He led them, by night, into the few farms that might supply hay and corn and garden stuff for troops. His years of watching helplessly while the Anglos took over the country that his own family had pioneered had not been wasted.

He would pause, pointing out a thickly wooded bend in the narrow track. "This it is perfect for ambush," he would say. Or, "You lie in wait here, soon you will catch someone who come to water his horse. Quick, one shot, then you are deep in the forest and no one know who or where."

That was the kind of thing Johnny had known he must learn, but he had never thought to be so lucky as to find someone so knowledgeable who might join him. As Jorge indicated such locations, Johnny's busy mind matched tasks to those of his companions who were best fitted to do them.

Luke, he thought, would be perfect for picking off single riders stopped at waterholes. Hidden well in the underbrush, he could remain safe, for he would be assigned only to lone soldiers carrying dispatches.

* * * * * * *

While Johnny and Jorge planned their campaigns, the women were making respectable widow's weeds for Hassie Mae. Ma had a long tongue and used it sometimes unwisely. It seemed sensible to let Hassie be their rich widow, accompanied by her maid Manuela. As Jorge assured them, nobody who had seen Manuela in the wood could ever recognize this neat, bright-eyed young woman as his outcast daughter.

Luke would go too, as Hassie's war-crippled brother. As such, he could purchase ammunition, weapons, and other items like more blasting powder, which would be useful when their own store was gone. They mended his clothing and found among Ma's relics in the wagon a jacket and hat that were suitable for his new part.

Summer was burning down on the river bottoms on the morning when the three set out in the trap for their first expedition to Nacogdoches. As it was considerably farther, and there were even more creeks to cross on the way, this would take far longer than the trip into San Augustine.

The year had been a wet one, even so far into fall, and the fords were muddy, as Johnny and Jorge had learned in their investigations. Double wheel tracks, rutted hub-deep, formed the road. In places, wagons had turned aside from mired spots, time after time, until great semicircles of muddy tracks bracketed outward from the worst areas.

Jorge, Mugual, and Senaqua reported much traffic on the road, so the three waited until the track was empty before pulling Turk out into the road. Johnny saw them go with a feeling of emptiness. He knew he was going to worry until they hove into sight again.

While the expedition was away, those remaining in the woods set about preparing alternate refuges, in case of hot pursuit. To pin all their hopes on this one camp was suicidal, Johnny thought, and Senaqua agreed.

"My people, while lacking in many of the refinements of civilization, are infinitely superior to yours in their ability to change at once and without bewailing the loss of material possessions," the Comanche said. "There is no spot that we cannot abandon instantly and without a backward glance. That is the reason we have managed to survive the encroachments of your kind as long as we have done. If you are to do the same, you must be able to go at once, leaving behind everything but your lives."

Johnny and Magda knew that, of course, though each dreaded still another disruption of their lives. However, they moved away through the forest, searching for suitable camp spots that would be inaccessible to searchers.

Both Comanche moved to the north and northwest. Luke stumped away on his crutches to the south along the river, following the game tracks along the bank, for the forest floor was difficult for crutches.

Napier mounted his big horse and went due west, and so clever was the animal, so deft his rider, that Johnny could not hear the sound of their passing once they had left his field of vision. Once he was out of sight, Johnny moved to the southwest, and the dogs ranged through the woods along his track. No matter how politely they acknowledged the rest of the band, their master was Johnny, as Absalom had told them.

It was Sue who gave warning. Johnny was in a small clearing, surveying the roll of the land toward the river and the screen of bushes and trees to the north and west. A chilly nose was thrust into his hand from behind, startling him, and he turned to look down into the bitch's red-brown eyes.

Certain that she had his attention, she turned her long head to stare eastward. Her ears pricked forward, and an all but inaudible growl trembled in her deep chest. She looked up again, as if to make certain he understood.

Johnny moved into the shelter of the hickory wood behind him, and the dog flickered away into the shadows of the forest. He was hard put to follow her as she angled toward the river.

Midnight drifted out of a shadowy clump of young sweetgum and came to Johnny's heel. With dogs fore and aft, he went quietly through the trees. In a few moments, he heard a sound of voices, and the clink of metal on metal.

Johnny sank into a button willow thicket edging the river bank, and the dogs faded into the brush as if they had never existed. Downriver, following the game track paralleling the water, were three horsemen, uniformed. Bluecoats, heading upstream.

Johnny surveyed the riverbank. Twenty yards from his position was a bluff, and the river had undercut it, as Jorge had shown him some time before. Below was an eddy that looked deep. There the trees grew close to the edge, and the horses would have to step carefully along the narrow path between forest and the rim of the drop to the river. It was a perfect spot for an ambush. Yet even with the help of the dogs, Johnny couldn't quite determine how one man, unaided, could force three horsemen over the bluff. He crawled backward through the undergrowth into the shelter of the deeper hickory dell and turned to find Jorge standing in the shadow, smiling his enigmatic half-smile.

Johnny looked down to find Sue at his knee. "Go find Midnight," he said.

She cocked an ear, wagged her long tail, and sped away toward the river. In two minutes she was back with her mate.

Johnny found it strange explaining a plan of action to a pair of dogs, but that is exactly what he did. While Jorge kept an eye on the three horsemen, he put it as plainly as he could. Looking into those bright dark eyes, he knew that they understood, to some extent, what he had told them.

The riders were checking out the country, pausing to listen and look off across the river or into the woods as they came. The sounds of their voices became louder, the clink of their gear more pronounced.

Johnny looked at Jorge, and the pair took up their posts as the dogs disappeared into the brush, waiting for their cue.

The sun was well above the treetops beyond the river when the three approached the chosen spot. They were alert, but they seemed not to know they were being watched as they moved into the ambush. When all the horses were strung out on the bluff, separated by a few yards, Johnny and his companion took aim and fired, their rifles cracking together in one blast of sound.

Before the first and the last man had fallen, the two dogs were upon the third, taking him with them over the edge into the deep eddy below. So sudden had been the attack that only that single volley needed to be fired. Not one of the victims had time to cry out.

While Jorge picked his way down to the eddy, Johnny caught the horses, which were snorting and dancing with fear, and led them into the forest. There he tied them securely to the hickory trees and soothed them before leaving. When he went to join Jorge, they were quiet, only whiffling softly through distended nostrils.

The two who had been shot were quite dead, one head shot, the other with his throat torn out by the slug, taking with it his jugular. The third was lying below on the sand bar edging the eddy.

Jorge looked up as he came. "I held him under until he drowned," he said. "It saved one shot, *es verdad*?"

"True enough," Johnny replied, reaching for a sodden blue sleeve.

They pulled the dead men out of the pool and across the sand bar, into the full current of the river. When they released each of them, the bodies went rolling down the stream, hanging up, from time to time, on logs or clumps of drift.

"They will float down to the great bend," said Jorge. "There they will hang up on all the dead trees and logs that came down the river in winter. The crawfish and the alligators will feast well, no? And no man will ever know what became of them."

That was the only farewell the unfortunate men ever had spoken over them.

It took a long time to backtrack the three, brushing away the tracks of the horses from the dusty path and the damp spots where creeks wandered down to the larger stream. The two cleaned clay banks marked by their passing, knowing that if Yankees came looking for their fellows there must be no trace they had ever come this way.

By the time they were done, the sun was moving down the west, beyond the thick canopy of branches. They collected the mounts and led them back to the cabin over thick mats of fallen leaves.

It was dark by the time they arrived, and Ma and the rest were already eating their supper of catfish and roast raccoon. They had found, with the help of the Garcías, that the forest ran over with food for those who knew how to find it.

And that was the first day. Even while settling on other locations for camps and beginning to put them into order, Johnny worried quietly about the three who were even now probably just arriving in Nacogdoches. But he kept busy and refused to say anything of what he felt.

Five and a half days after leaving, the trap returned with all aboard who had left in it. The scanty storage box at the back of the rig was crammed with goods. Wrapped bundles surrounded the feet of the passengers.

Turk whinnied with pleasure at rejoining his friends in the patch beside the river, and those he brought behind him seemed happy to get home again.

Fresh fillets of fat channel catfish were put sizzling into the long-handled skillet, the coffee pot was filled, and the expedition members unloaded their booty as the food cooked. Boxes of ammunition were in the box. Rifles and handguns with U.S. Army markings were in the long bundles concealed behind the women's long skirts.

Dried fruit and cornmeal and coffee (they had been getting woefully low on that) were packed in with other supplies of all kinds. There were nails and chain, harness parts and a handsaw, hammer, and crosscut.

"Gold goes a mighty long way, sure enough," said Hassie, coming out of the cabin in her old serge skirt and cotton blouse. She sighed with satisfaction. "I am almighty glad to be out of those widow's weeds! In this heat, that black material will cook you alive."

She took her place between Manuela and Luke and accepted a loaded plate and a cup of coffee. "You would have been proud of Luke here," she managed to say around a mouthful of catfish.

"He made about the most pitiful cripple you ever want to see. His 'stiff upper lip' act was worth the price of admission, and the way he dealt with the storekeepers—I can only say it was masterful the way he managed that.

"He spent what money he had to without ever letting anybody suspect that we might have more. You'd have thought we were going to starve, if he spent too much on the necessaries."

She began to laugh, choked, and regained her breath. "And when that Yankee Captain started asking questions, he was slick as a greased weasel!"

She lifted her fork and turned to Luke. "You tell about it, will you Luke?" she said. "I've got to eat or drop flat."

Luke grinned, and Johnny leaned back against a tree trunk to enjoy the tale.

CHAPTER TWENTY-SIX

Luke stretched lazily, his peg leg supporting his good one. He took a sip of coffee and glanced at Johnny, his grin fading as his eyes met those of his leader.

"You know that Yank Captain you've told us about?" he began. "I knew that he couldn't possibly be the only bastard in the Union Army, but we seem to have one in Nacogdoches that runs him a close race for Bastard-in-Chief. The one in charge over there is so full of himself that he's spilling over."

Johnny leaned forward and poured the dregs of his coffee onto the fire. "What does he look like?" he asked.

"Face like a hacksaw," said Luke. "Cold eyes, pale ones. Sandy-gray hair, what I could see beneath his cap. He is very tall and thin, and I noticed on his hand a heavy gold ring with a crest engraved on it."

Johnny felt his interior chill and glanced over at Magda. Her jaw was set, her eyes matching any coldness the Captain might manage. He knew that she was seeing, even as he was, the heavy ring on the hand that had been raised to signal the hanging of their parents.

"He was supposed to go someplace west. San Saba?" Magda asked.

Luke chuckled without humor. "The one thing about any army that never changes is that everything always changes. Orders, plans, commanders, posts. He might have had his orders changed after you chewed up his command.

Nacogdoches is probably a pretty low prestige post, with nobody much left here but women and children and a few ex-slaves. The menfolk are just now beginning to drift back from wherever they were when the war ended. The Indians have moved farther west, and nothing much is a threat here."

Johnny sighed, staring at the coals. "So he is going to be angry as a wet wasp. Doing everything he can to get even with the world. What did he do to you?"

"Not much, really, considering. But oh, how he wanted to! We had been in town a day and part of the next. I was in the hardware section of the store, picking out leather and bits of harness, while the women were finding the food supplies.

"The storekeeper must have pointed me out to the officer, for he came marching across the store and stood staring at me as if I might be some sort of vermin." Luke grinned.

"It's a very good thing I am not wanted anywhere, for he seemed to be running my face through a long list of wanted posters. His mental files were going over them; you could see it in his eyes."

He poured his own coffee dregs on the ground and set the tin cup neatly on the stump beside him. "'Who are you and what are you doing here?' he asked me, as if he expected me to spring to attention like a mossy-eared private.

"I looked him straight in the eyes and said, 'I am Luke Cornwall. I am here with my sister, and we're going to farm back east of here. We need equipment to get started, and what the hell business is it of yours?'

"He looked as if he would like to bite my ears off and spit them in my face. I could see the storekeeper off in the corner trying to keep a straight face. The Captain could see him too, from the angle he was standing, and that didn't go down well at all. So I turned my back and walked off to the nail barrels."

Hassie chuckled. "He missed the best part, when he turned his back. That man looked as if he had been slapped with a wet fish. He tore across the store after Luke, and I yelled for him to look out. Luke turned and seemed to lose his balance, and that wooden leg went out at just the right angle." A giggle escaped her.

"The Captain took a header right over it and into a pile of horse collars. The storekeeper had to go off into the back of the store, and I was laughing aloud. Two ladies out front saw enough to make them have a fit of the giggles, and that Captain will never, ever, forgive us.

"If he could have thought of a complaint that could stick, he'd have arrested the three of us and thrown us into the jail. But what could he do to a poor bereaved woman and her one-legged brother? We are not on any list any-place, and to all the witnesses it was obvious everything that happened was an accident." Hassie laid her plate aside and folded her hands on her lap.

"He dogged our steps the rest of our time in town. It's good we had the guns and ammunition already, or we would have had to wait for them, because he would have been terribly suspicious.

"We made it a point not to hurry away, so he wouldn't think we were trying to avoid him. We'd have been here yesterday, if we had come straight on in. The roads are drying out in the heat, and the fords are getting solid.

"So." Johnny looked about the circle of faces, red-lit by the coals of the dying fire. "Now we have supplies. We will put stores of them at our alternate camps. We have extra mounts Jorge and I lucked into a couple the other day.

"I wonder if Absalom would hide them for us, in case we need them in a hurry and can't get back here to the pen?" He looked at Jorge, who nodded.

The long face was expressionless. "*Sí.* Absalom has grassland behind his house. It cannot be seen from the river or from any road. Indeed, no roads run anywhere near Absalom's home.

"He burns off the spot so the deer will come and browse. He hunts for his food, and he is growing old. It is easier if the game is nearby. If we build some sort of pen to keep the beasts from wandering, yes. I believe yes."

Johnny gave a long sigh. He had waited and worked, traveling long miles to reach this point. The people were ready now.

But since the time had arrived, he found himself having qualms. The Yankees deserved all the hell he could give them, but some of these willing souls might suffer and die because he had a vision of vengeance. Would his vendetta kill his friends?

He shook off the feeling of depression. "Now our war will begin," he said, and no voice was raised in protest.

*   *   *   *   *   *   *

They rose the next morning ready to begin. Napier rode toward the Camino Real, prepared to watch any traffic closely for several days. He took with him supplies for a week.

Jorge went to alert Absalom. Luke and Johnny went through the weapons and ammunition, piece by piece. They cleaned the rifles and pistols and even Ma's shotgun. They measured powder and lead and percussion caps for the older weapons and parceled out cartridges for the newer ones captured from the three Yankees by the river. They found themselves with a mixed bag of weaponry, counting that brought from Nacogdoches. Matching the right loads for each, they assigned them to the individuals best suited to using them.

Mugual ranged the woods, more from restlessness than from any real fear of searchers, leaving his father to oversee the weapons-check. Senaqua did not look well. His usual coppery shade had an ashy undertone, and while he did not move stiffly, he carried himself a bit too carefully for one with his stoicism.

Johnny feared that he had not recovered as well from his wounds as he pretended. It told him much that the Comanche had not volunteered to go out on an investigative foray, this first morning of their war. He did take part in sorting the ammunition into the cotton bags Ma had made for the purpose. His eyes were thoughtful and his hands quick, as he said, "I have had a thought. Something so unusual and unthreatening that it cannot possibly alarm even your Captain.

"It could pull in enough people to make the troops concentrate their strength in Nacogdoches for several days." He stared down at his busy hands. "Why not put on a circus?"

Johnny stared at him, dumbfounded. "A circus?"

Potesenaquahip nodded. "You and your sister have the skills. Mugual is becoming quite accomplished, as well. Ma is not known in the town, and she could provide... comic relief." There was a wicked twinkle in the black eyes.

"Napier would make a fine ringmaster, and Luke could sit in a booth and take in the admissions. I..."—he looked incredibly dignified—"...could tell fortunes."

Johnny felt a surge of excitement as he turned to look at Luke.

Senaqua was not yet done. "It is probable that without her widow's weeds, Hassie Mae will not be recognized. She says that she kept her veil down when in public. Not one of us will be expected to be here, and far less will we be looked for in such unlikely company.

"It is true that we have no spangles and tights, but nowadays this would not be expected, I think. We have the trained ponies, and they perform on cue, as we all know. With music—Napier can be our orchestra as well as ringmaster—they will be quite content."

Johnny found the possibilities intriguing. And how appropriate it would be to avenge themselves on the murderer of their own circus by means of another one. He grinned at the Comanche.

"I think you are right," he said.

"Me, too," said Luke. "Makes a lot of sense. If we just pick off singles at fords and along the roads, they will begin coming in such numbers that it will make that impossible. But if we have a whole bunch together, and if we can get them at one stroke, that will be excellent. We will disappear into the woods at once, and the risk will be no more and possibly much less."

The women, skinning squirrels at the board table they had strung between two trees, had been listening. Magda now said, "It will work, I think. Did you know that Manuela dances? We can make one more trip to town after fancy goods. A Spanish lace shawl, some shiny stuff for costumes, beads.

"Without the rigging, we can't do the trapeze act, but we can do trick riding and knife-throwing and acrobatics and juggling. I think it is a very good plan, Senaqua."

"We could plan three performances," Johnny said, as much to himself as the others. "Thursday night, Friday night, Saturday afternoon. The first two shows will be talked about all over the country. Word will spread through the countryside like a forest fire.

"By then the troops will be used to our presence, not expecting anything worse than a drunk shooting off a pistol in public. On Saturday afternoon, it will be time to hit them." He thought for a moment.

Then he sighed. "That would be the best way. But it might be wisest to limit ourselves to a single performance. For safety."

"What about the people? The women and children who will come to the show? We don't want to kill any of them!" Magda objected.

"We will wait until the show is over. The crowd can disperse and start home. We shall take our time about breaking down the ring and getting the animals ready to move, and that will be the time...." Johnny found himself warming to the subject.

"When I was in France, I saw men from the East," said Senaqua. "They were much like Mugual and me, except for their clothing. We might make turbans and robes like those I remember. It would be most unusual for Indians to be involved in a circus, and we should never be suspected of being anything except Swamis from afar. What do you think of that?"

Hassie Mae came over and knelt beside him. "I saw one once. Came through Alatosa—you remember, Ma? Had on white robes like the ones in your big Bible. His head was wrapped up in bright cloth, with a little cone sticking out the top. We could make you and Mugual look just like him!"

Ma put the cleaned squirrels into the pot over the open fire and washed her hands in the nearby bucket. "We can. And it sounds like rip-roaring fun to me. Anybody can go dashing in and shoot up a town and get away and be just one more mean bunch. Nobody I ever heard about ever went in as a circus and left as an army. Let's do it."

They were all getting excited, Johnny could see. Nobody had been completely satisfied with the hit-and-run tactics they had been planning. This, however, seemed ideal for their purposes.

While they talked and planned and measured for costumes and cut rope and straps for rigging, Jorge came out of the trees. He was carrying Absalom, who had a bloody bandage about his dark head.

Midnight and Sue dashed worriedly between their old master and their new one, growling softly. Johnny stooped to pet their heads as he called for Ma.

In minutes the women had the old black stretched on their work table, stitching up the long gash in his scalp. That wasn't as easy as it sounded, for blood surged from the wound in endless amounts. And when they turned him to search for other injuries, he moaned with anguish.

"Ribs," said Ma. "Broken. And a lot of bruises. He's most spongy with 'em. What in tunket happened to the poor old fellow, Jorge?"

"Yankees," said the Spaniard. "For no reason. They say we must free the Negro, and they make a war they say is for that. Now they beat him, old as he is, just because he is black and alone. I do not understand *Anglos*."

"What about his dogs?" asked Johnny.

"Many they kill. There are dead dogs all about his house. They come to protect him, the soldiers shoot them. There are more, I think in the wood, but until he come to himself and call, we will not know. They will not show themselves to us without his permission."

Johnny moved to the table and stared down at the elderly man. The eyes opened, glazed and bruised-looking between swollen lids.

"Now," said Absalom, "I sure to God will help you fight 'em."

CHAPTER TWENTY-SEVEN

Absalom was badly bruised, his collarbone broken, and Johnny thought that his old bones might well have shattered under the beating they had taken. But the man was tough and tenacious, and as soon as he was salved with Mama's special ointment and bandaged well, he seemed anxious to enter into any plans the group might be making.

"We're going to put on a horse and dog show, with acrobats and clowns," Ma told him, helping him to sit and lean against a rolled blanket. "And if you're the man who trained our two dogs, you can do wonders with 'em, once you're able. We could put together a classy act with dogs and ponies, if any of your bunch of critters is still out there in the brush."

Absalom blinked hard and shook his head. "What she talking about?" he asked Johnny, who had dropped onto a chunk of wood beside the old man.

"We will tell you about it when you're better," Johnny told him. "Don't worry about it right now. But once you feel yourself again, we have a project in mind that you may enjoy."

Jorge, who knew nothing, as yet, of the plan, quirked an eyebrow at Johnny, but he agreed. "Wait. We will find you a spot and build you a shelter, as we have done for ourselves. And then we will see."

It took a couple of days for Absalom to get about again, but his mind was clear and acute much sooner. The next morning, in fact, he braced Johnny again.

And once the strategy was explained to him, the old man was enthusiastic. "If you is going to fight a war, then by gum why not fight one that's fun?" he asked.

"No way could them Yankees kill all my dogs. I done train 'em to run like hell when folks shoots at 'em. You just wait—I can have the doggonedest dog act you ever did see."

The thing they had to wait for was his lips to lose their swelling enough to pucker a whistle for the animals lurking in the forest. His lips resembled dark balloons for some time, and he fretted about it. But they kept asking his advice about their proposed circus, and he took great delight in the tumbling and juggling and trick riding that the younger people were practicing.

Johnny and Mugual had devised a portable ring like that with movable sections the old Gannelli Family Circus had carried about with them. Magda had taken charge of making trappings for the horses and ponies, and by the time those were well begun, Absalom was able to whistle.

When his shrill notes rang out through the trees, dogs began slipping into view like ghosts. Johnny knew that the animals had been watching the camp and their master closely all the while, though not one of his group—unless, indeed, it might be Midnight or Sue—had caught a glimpse of one.

Only eight were left of the twenty dogs Absalom had finished training and allowed to roam the wood about his house. They were clear-eyed and alert, as were Sue and Midnight, and they understood training quickly and followed signals intelligently.

Johnny and his companions set up the ring in the clearing before the cabin. Napier took out his harmonica and tried a trill. Then he struck up one of the familiar airs, and the ponies raised their heads and snorted delicately.

With seeming delight, the pair trotted into the ring and took up their rhythmic pacing around its circle. The old wagon horse was too staid to rebel, and soon it, too, had learned the pace, and Turk seemed not to mind having a young woman on tiptoe on his ridged back.

Once they had the animals back into training, Johnny and Magda sharpened their old skills again, leaping from back to back, riding one-footed, and switching from ground to horseback to handstand with smoothness and ease.

However, it was Mugual who seemed likely to steal the show. His long Indian hair hidden by a turban made from towels, he looked either Egyptian or Assyrian, as his lithe young body flowed from horse to horse, up and down.

He flipped and leaped and did handstands as if he had been born a true Gannelli. Senaqua, sitting quietly, hands busy with costumes or equipment, allowed his expression to take on entirely un-Indian pride, as Johnny noted with amusement.

Johnny had never been the trick rider that Magda had, preferring the knives or the trapeze, so he gladly relinquished his place to Mugual. Standing back to watch his cousin and her partner, he found them better than good. With proper costumes and surroundings, he felt that they soon might equal the best anywhere.

Matched fairly in size, they seemed able to read each other's minds as they traded places or as Magda took off in a soaring leap to stand on Mugual's shoulders. Once the dogs had begun their training, they found a smaller one, Tripper, that took to the pair, ending the act by scrambling up both riders to take his place draped around Magda's shoulders, his tail wagging furiously.

But it was the reaction of the ponies that surprised Johnny most. Absalom, through his language of whistles and grunts and finger-snaps, seemed able to convey to his dogs almost anything Johnny described to him. When they understood what they were to do, two of the dogs, small grays, began working with the ponies, and both parties seemed more than satisfied with the situation.

In the evenings, when the chores were completed and all were sitting around, well back from the heat of the fire, the circus rehearsals took place. Invariably, the dogs and ponies brought down the house, as the gray dogs moved daintily up and down their ramps, alighting on the moving backs as if they weighed no more than feathers.

The ponies, of course, never altered their pacing as the dogs rode, at first four-footed, then, with increasing skill, standing on their hind legs, front paws in the air. Both dogs and ponies looked as if they enjoyed the routine, and never did either species object to the presence of the other.

Six larger dogs were trained to leap over the ponies bodily, as they paced the ring. Racing outside the barrier, they would fling themselves into the air just as the ponies, their riders in place, moved past certain points.

As time passed and the fall began to wane, Johnny knew that they were nearing the point at which they could succeed with their plan. It was costumes that required much time and effort, before they could make their attempt.

Deciding that it might be too dangerous to go into town after such fripperies, Ma delved into her big trunk, which had been hauled all the way from Louisiana in the wagon and finally deposited in the cabin.

That contained her wedding dress, her mother's hand-made lace, and all manner of unwearable but treasured items that the old woman could not bear to leave behind when she left the farmhouse in which she and her husband had lived before going to care for his mother. It had been stored in an outbuilding and so had not been burned with the inn.

There were long strands of beads, a rainbow of bright scarves, and yards and yards of satin from the wedding dress. Costumes came into being that showed no signs of beginning life as wedding veils or alpaca coats or embroidered tablecloths.

Magda and Ma and Hassie Mae put their heads together over each set and came up with original and striking ideas. Mugual stood patiently, playing dressmaker's dummy with what Johnny considered remarkable aplomb, while the three cut and tucked and pinned.

When at last everything was finished, it was astonishing the variety and beauty of the outfits they had contrived. Each of the men had undergone fittings, suffering in silence as the others sat about and made life even more uncomfortable with rude remarks. Only Senaqua seemed unruffled.

He was distinguished looking in his long gray robe and white turban. A shawl of rainbow embroidery draped his shoulders, making him look like some prophet out of the Old Testament.

Of course, the circus was not created in a day or a week. Training animals to work together and getting a slick, professional sequence of acts devised and rehearsed could not be rushed. No element, whether style of performance or quality of costume, could be slighted or rushed.

But before winter put a stop to their plan, they were ready.

Down in the river bottoms, life did not become easier for them. Insects made their days and nights miserable; everyone except the Indians suffered desperately from mosquito bites on exposed and unexposed skins alike.

However, not one of the whites could bear the Indian remedy, rubbing themselves with opossum-fat, as the Comanche did. The smell, in hot weather, was enough to insure both Mugual and Senaqua all the privacy they might want and plenty of elbow room. They had to wash it off in the river before donning their costumes for rehearsals.

The weeks of work had produced a professional-looking circus, for the time and the area. It satisfied even the Gannellis' exacting eyes, and though he never mentioned it to his cousin, Johnny felt that his father and mother must be looking over his shoulder all the time, nodding approval or frowning at a mishap.

This was being done for them and for Celie and Barnabas. It would be fitting for them all to take an interest, wherever their spirits might be, in the progress of this new circus.

At last Hassie-Mae had to go into town to get paint and board for posters. No self-respecting circus comes to town without advance fanfare; they had to advertise, they all knew.

Luckily, things went well, and the Captain, though he noted her coming and going with obvious attention, did not inquire into the nature of the "widow's" purchases. She and Manuela returned with enough material to suffice.

Johnny and Magda had helped to paint many a circus poster, and their experience speeded up the process of creating their own. Once they decided on a name for the show, which was not an easy task, the rest was easy.

Of course it was impossible to call it the Gannelli Family Circus. The Captain, if he was, indeed, the one Johnny thought, would know it at once.

Devinney hadn't quite that true circus ring to it. At last they decided to call it after Senaqua's "circus" name, Hashi Ben Ali. The Hashi Ben Ali Combined Shows.

Heaven knew, Johnny chuckled, that this was an odd combination of many kinds, races, individuals, and grudges. The title was an accurate one, besides being foreign and exotic enough to rouse the interest of these entertainment starved backwoods people.

By night, Johnny and Mugual slipped into Nacogdoches and nailed posters to trees, posts, and fences. Nobody saw them, and Johnny knew that it would seem magical when the townsfolk woke to find the bright signs sprouted overnight on their quiet street.

They gave the advertising a week to percolate through the town and its environs. They gave it another to pull in all available troops to keep order, which Luke assured them would be done. The occupying force was as bored as everyone else in the area.

Then they hitched up ponies and horses to the strange array of wheeled vehicles they had cobbled together from found materials and decorated with the remains of the paint. They marched into Nacogdoches to the sound of drums (created by Absalom from deer hide and barrel hoops) and the lively strains of Napier's harmonica.

Down the steep, wooded hill east of town they came, over the rickety bridge that crossed the Banita Creek, and up the hill into the tiny downtown area, toward the bend in the road guarded by the combination fort and store/saloon.

Their own mothers would never have recognized any of them. Napier's face stared at him from a wall of wanted posters as he passed. Johnny saw him smile beneath the horsehair moustache. He kept on playing,

The circus had come to town at last!

CHAPTER TWENTY-EIGHT

As they banged and rattled up the rutted street, Johnny found himself marveling at the appearance and the style his group managed to muster. Not one was recognizable. He had grown a full beard, and Ma had fashioned him a piratical outfit that suited his black hair, beard, and moustache.

Magda's hair had grown back, and she had piled it high on her head, bound with strands of beads from an old portiere of Ma's. It would stay solidly in place as she bounced and spun, and her cousin felt that the Captain had not had a good look at the girl, anyway. His attention had been on Johnny, when they had originally encountered the officer.

Ma was swathed in several veils, which hid her serge skirt. Her head was bound up in a blowsy turban that lent her a rakish and somewhat dangerous air. It had taken little persuasion to get her to become a clown, and she had an inborn knack for the part.

In the next vehicle (two wheels from an abandoned farm had been its basis) rode the Comanche, with all the contained dignity of a pair of patriarchs just stepped out of the Old Testament. Manuela drove the horse and nobody, knowing her before, would ever have recognized her as the girl driven from her home with her father.

Forrest Napier rode a horse (heavily disguised with paint and draped saddle). He played the harmonica from time to time, as needed, and Johnny chuckled every time he noticed that flowing horsehair moustache. Napier had tried his best to grow his own, but his facial hair grew in tufts that did nothing to disguise him. They just looked comical.

Luke was dressed soberly as a roustabout, his beard dyed darker and trimmed differently than it had been when he visited the town. But no bright colors called attention to him. Johnny wanted no curious glances to size him up and remember the brother of that rich widow.

Absalom drove the trap, which had been heavily disguised with the removal of its bonnet-like hood and the addition of a sort of "boot" at the rear made of boxes holding the parts of the ring. His equipage got more attention than any, for the old man was in full African regalia, as nearly as the group could come to imagining it. His facial decorations were done in a mix of ochre and bear grease. An upright headdress of horsetail was ornamented with flowers from a hat that had belonged to Ma's mother.

The dogs, each wearing a collar made of ribbon rosettes, marched quietly alongside the vehicle. Not one of them deigned to notice the small boys calling rude remarks and pitching pebbles at their heels.

Jorge they did not risk in their parade. He was well known to the older inhabitants of the town, and it was considered wisest to station him in the forest east of Nacogdoches. With him were their arsenal and the extra mounts. When the time came, his part would decide the success or failure of their raid.

Johnny rode in a sort of dogcart scrounged from bits and pieces found in raids on trash heaps and city dumps. It was coated with bright paint and pulled by Turk, and behind Johnny Hassie Mae stood braced against the seat. She was adorned in every bit of colorful finery they could fit onto her, her light hair braided and puffed, threaded with a string of pearl beads Ma found at the bottom of that capacious trunk. Across her chest was a banner that said

DAME FORTUNE

A rather sketchy rendition of the *Poet and Peasant Overture*, as arranged for harmonica and drums, struck up as soon as they had crossed the creek. They came up through the approach to the downtown area amid a clatter of hooves, the snorting of the ponies, and shrill giggles from all the children running alongside the procession.

Along the dusty street, wagons and buggies and saddle horses were tied to hitching posts. More children darted across the road like schools of minnows, risking their lives among the horses and between the feet of adults more intent upon the circus than what was beneath their boots.

Straggles of skinny, sunburned people lined the way, with smiling Negroes and wailing babies and yapping curs seasoning the mix. Between the halves of the crowd, they came into a space, in the middle of which was a wide area with some large oaks and even more vehicles that were hitched around it.

Luke and Napier peeled off toward the site they had secretly chosen for setting up the ring, while the others circled the square, drums thumping rhythmically. By the time the parade headed for the circus area, the two men had the parts of the ring up, the ramps in place, and more banners and posters hung from trees and nailed onto posts.

Napier was a ringmaster to rival even Papa Gannelli. He had a flair for it, there was no mistaking it. While the performers were changing into other costumes, he kept the audience spellbound with accounts of the wonders they were about to see.

At last the dogs came trotting into the ring, bows springing brightly at each neck. Napier bowed, taking out his harmonica, and the circus began as the ponies came in and went into their regular pacing.

The bigger dogs scampered up their ramps and leaped over the little beasts, while the grays bounced onto their backs, on and off again as if they had been doing that all their lives. From the sidelines, clicks from Absalom's fingers or short whistles guided their actions unobtrusively. The audience exploded into applause when they trooped out of the ring, disappearing behind the canvas wall erected to conceal costume changes and resting performers.

When Manuela stepped out of concealment in her flounced dress, clicking her fingers (for lack of castanets), she immediately held the attention of the audience. She tapped her heels on the small board floor put there for her, her body curving and pirouetting as she danced. She was so good that she brought howls of appreciation from some of the troops watching among the crowd.

Magda and Mugual came out next, and the ponies returned. The pair were so well matched, so smooth and effortless in their leaps and catches, their bounds and somersaults to horseback that Johnny felt a twinge of jealousy as he watched them.

Then came his turn, and he faced the whirling marks, his knives flashing from his hands, snicking into the moving targets. Magda flung him blazing torches, and he proceeded to juggle those without singeing his mustachios. While the troopers were not as enthusiastic, the farmers and their wives and children made up for that as he took his bows and retired.

Ma followed him, dressed as a clown in a billowing dress and flowing veils, which flapped in the breeze of her movement. She chased Hassie with an improvised rolling pin, her wildly painted face grimacing demonically. She threatened Johnny and the ringmaster, and they picked her up and stuffed her into a barrel. The audience all but rolled on the grass. Ma was a born comedienne.

As she was rolled behind the curtain, still in her barrel, Senaqua and Mugual, in their robes and turbans, came out. Napier gestured toward the pair, bowing low.

"I have the inestimable honor of introducing Hashi Ben Ali and his acolyte. This mage of the mysterious East will, for a modest consideration, consult with any who feel the need of counseling. Trained in the ancient mysteries of the Orient, he knows what has been and what will be, the past, the present, and the future."

He straightened and faced Senaqua. "Oh wise and benevolent Hashi, what is it that you see in store for this city and its citizens?"

The Comanche stared around the audience, his dignity almost tangible. Then his commanding voice rolled forth in a long and unintelligible soliloquy. Johnny recognized the language as German, for Cousin Barnabas came from a large German family before marrying Cousin Celie.

To the crowd, it must have sounded like the authentic tongue of the djinn, so blankly did they stare at the solemn speaker.

"That, my friends, is the language of prophecy," said Napier. "Once you come to speak privately with this wonderful soothsayer, his acolyte will translate for you the words he has spoken, as well as others that may apply directly to your own lives and welfare. He will, I assure you, learn wonderful things behind the Veil."

The Comanche slipped behind the curtain, and Magda emerged in her brief tumbling costume. She rolled around the ring, a bright cartwheel, before going into an intricate set of handsprings, tumbles, and stretches.

Her acrobatic skill, Johnny knew, was not appreciated nearly as much as the elegance of her legs. More than one stern matriarch held a work-rough hand over the eyes of more than one small boy, as his cousin went through her performance. Mugual, again in his tumbling costume, joined the girl, and the pair flipped and twirled their bodies through the air, twisting into impossible positions and out again, ending with Magda standing upright on the boy's shoulders.

When they were done, Johnny began climbing the pole they had braced into the ground. He set his wrist into the loop at the top and began spinning in larger and larger circles from the top of the pole.

The sun was going down now, and as he spun, he spotted himself by the shadow of the pole across the ground below. When the shadow was obscured by the trees edging the field, he slowed to a stop and dropped onto the ground again, accompanied by hysterical applause. He wondered how many small boys would be treated for broken wrists in the next few weeks.

Intermission was declared, while customers had their consultations with Hashi Ben Ali. The rest made trips to nearby wells and privies or to the bushes edging the ridge where the town had been set.

Johnny watched intently. All the soldiers seemed to be in good humor, unsuspicious and out for a good time. The other people laughed and jostled and were relaxed and happy. Perhaps things would work out just as they had hoped.

When the Comanche had finished with his last client, the troop paraded a last time around the ring amid the long shadows of evening. Children were already whining, coming out of the spell cast by this undreamed of entertainment.

One by one the performers retired behind the canvas curtain, as Napier gave a farewell spiel from the center of the ring. Magda kept watch through a convenient slit in the curtain, keeping Johnny informed of the movements of audience and soldiers.

They removed their costumes hastily and donned their own rough clothing, listening to her continuing reports. "They are chasing off a bunch of little boys now," Magda said. "The little devils were trying to get onto one of the ponies. Poor old Pietro has done his work for the day, and he didn't like that a bit. He tried to kick."

Ma, looking completely respectable now in her old serge and bonnet, joined the girl at the slit. "Looks as if the last have gone now," she said. "Johnny, are we ready to strike the ring and the curtain?"

"If we delay any longer, someone will be suspicious. But do it slowly," he said, "as if you are very tired."

She snorted. "Lord, boy, who isn't tired? You got old bones like mine sashaying around dressed up like the Queen of Sheba, and you can bet they're going to holler 'Uncle' pretty fast."

Johnny turned to grin at the old woman. "Well, act tireder than you look. Is everyone ready?"

They straggled out of the shelter and began loosing knots, coiling ropes, dismantling the ring. They hitched up the animals to the different carts and lined up the rigs and the animals. It took little acting to convey the impression that they were an exhausted group, ready for nothing but rest.

They finished up as the sun set. Johnny glanced up to see a man standing beneath one of the big pines at the edge of the field. He was watching them, there was no doubt of it. Something about his stance, the set of his head on his shoulders, was damnably familiar.

Magda turned to speak, saw the watcher, and turned pale. Her breath hissed inward, but before she could speak, Johnny touched her shoulder and shook his head.

"I see him," he said in a conversational tone. "Don't pay any attention, just get into the cart with Luke. It's time to go. Time to get this new show on the road."

She sighed, her breath ragged in her throat. "I'm tired to death, but the sight of that...that beast fills me with energy again. I had not realized that anger could wash away weariness, but it does. I am more than ready, *Caro*."

They climbed into carts and onto mounts, their motions slow and deliberate. A taggle of small boys hid in the brush, watching, but Johnny ignored them. He turned his mount's head toward the east, as they moved through the twilit streets, and he felt on his back the gaze of that officer beneath the pine tree.

Absalom gave a long whistle, and the dogs, freed of their unaccustomed finery, moved into place flanking the old man's wagon. Johnny turned in his saddle to check the entourage. Everyone was in place.

Night was coming. Jorge was in place, waiting outside of town in the forest.

He raised his hand. "Let's go," said Gian-Carlo Gannelli.

CHAPTER TWENTY-NINE

It was dark as they topped the hill and followed the winding track into the corridor of tall trees. The lanterns had been lighted, for no moonlight could find its way between the layered branches except in faint drifts and spatters.

Mugual shrugged off his shirt and removed the scarf that disguised his Comanche hair. Now he dropped off the wagon where he rode beside his father and slipped back down the road to watch their back trail. His keen young ears would detect anything that moved in the night.

The horses and ponies were weary. Even the dogs drooped as they moved like shadows beside Absalom's cart wheels. Johnny heard their soft panting as he rode along in the faint jingle of harness and the sound of hooves thudding into deep dust.

Three miles from town, Jorge waited with the weapons, along with bear grease mixed with ashes to spread on their skins, disguising the white members of the troupe. An attack by "Indians," which though unexpected by the locals would be theoretically possible, might deflect attention from the circus until they could disappear into the forest again to wait for another chance to attack their prey.

It took a long while to work their carts and horses into the thickets where Jorge was hidden, for they had to cover the track where they turned aside from the road. The lanterns pooled their light in a tiny clearing, shielded from any possible traveler by the forest and the bodies of two of the vehicles pulled together.

In that reddish light, the amateur guerrillas took turns rubbing the nasty mixture on the skin of the faces, hands, and necks of their fellows. Their hair was already long, and a bit of artistic work by Senaqua made them look authentic enough to fool a bunch of Yankees, particularly in darkness.

Their two Comanche could, they assured Johnny, provide war whoops enough to do justice to an entire tribe. Johnny hoped the deception would work, and he had a feeling that they were going to pull it off.

Even as he wondered why he didn't feel better about that, Magda came to stand beside him and took his hand. In the lantern light, she looked sad. He knew what she was thinking, as usual. Would Mama and Papa truly approve of killing other people, no matter what the provocation?

They stood together wordlessly. Ma, now a strange and horrifying spectre, came to join them. Her grizzled hair was bound about her forehead but sprang out below the band vigorously. She wore trousers, with a flapping shirt. She did not look like herself or like anything else ever seen by Man, Johnny thought.

She came right to the point. "I been thinking," she said. "You may feel as if I've taken my own sweet time about it, but I never claimed to be any great brain, and it takes a bit to get things straight in my mind."

Johnny held his breath, waiting for her to continue.

"I watched them Yankee boys while they was at the circus. They laughed and yelled and carried on like any bunch of young'uns away from home and lonesome. They're not monsters, Johnny. They're just kids. Come to think of it, it wasn't the Reb soldiers that caused our boarding house to burn. It was their triple-damned officers, and if I read your situation right, it was the same with your folks. The soldiers did what that officer told 'em to, didn't they?

"I just can't feel right about slaughtering those boys. How will we know whether they're privates or captains or what, there in the dark? I just don't feel right it don't set right in my craw, and that's the truth."

Johnny had known, on some deep level of his mind, what she was going to say. He had been thinking the same thing, though he kept pushing the thought away. He had no other reason to be uncomfortable, for all their plans had gone off perfectly. He drew a deep breath, feeling his nerves ease.

"You're right, Ma," Magda said, squeezing his hand. "I have been feeling the same, but I could not bring myself to admit it. Why should we kill a lot of innocent bystanders, when it is the Captain we want? We will be no better than he, if we go ahead with our original plan."

"But how in the name of all that's holy can we get him out alone?" asked Johnny.

At that moment, what he later decided had to be nothing but Providence took a hand in their affairs. Mugual slid into the light, his head cocked in a warning of danger.

There came a rapid grunting of Comanche between the pair of Indians, for Mugual tended to lose his English when he had other things on his mind. Senaqua stood up in the cart, where he had been lending a hand with the disguises of the other whites.

"We are being followed. A half mile back there are six men, led by your friend the Captain. They are on our track, Mugual is certain. They will miss our turn into the wood, for we hid it well and it is very dark on the road. White men are not good trackers, anyway.

"They will believe us to be ahead of them, still. If we should attack from the rear...." He smiled, his teeth a wicked glint of white in the dim light. "If any should survive, who among them would ever suspect that we might be the attackers?"

"The moon, it comes," said Mugual. "One hour, maybe, it is overhead. Ahead there is glade, and they will come there, unless they stop, as the moon is high. There will be light."

Senaqua, still standing on the cart, sighed. "I have been contaminated," he said, "by your culture. That is very strange, for it does not practice what it preaches by any means. Yet I find myself, Potesenaquahip, medicine chief, Comanche, unwilling to fall upon those unsuspecting people back there who are chuckling in their sleep over the show we provided for them. They have done us no wrong, and I feel a cold dislike of what we plan to do."

"White men shot you full of holes!" Luke objected, though he seemed to be struggling to hold down laughter. "I'd call that a considerable wrong, if it were my own skin involved."

The Comanche laughed deeply. "True. But I shot many of them full of holes as well, when they suspected no danger and had camped for the night. It was an even trade, with no hard feelings on either side. But now I find myself unwilling to continue that war. Indeed, I find that I like being a wise man from the mysterious East more than I ever liked being either a Comanche or a white man. It is a pity our circus days are over."

Johnny felt a surge of excitement well up inside him. He almost could hear the joyous notes of Papa's fiddle and Mama's accordion. He strode forward to stand beside the cart.

"But why should they be?" he asked, laughter in his voice. "Let's hit this bunch that has followed us, handed to us like a gift. Let us do what must be done to the Captain, who deserves worse than he is likely to get. And then let us go forward as a group. As a circus, indeed, everyone playing his part?" They could all hear the question in his voice.

A whisper circled the ash-smeared troupe. "Yes."

But there was no time to pursue that if they were to catch up to the troop as it reached the moonlit glade. They found their weapons, each taking that most suited to his skills, and mounted the horses, riding double when they ran short of steeds.

Jorge consulted with Mugual for a moment. Then the pair led the raiding party down a deer trail and along a creek paralleling the road.

Johnny followed confidently, knowing that between them the pair knew every inch of forest between Nacogdoches and the river. In single file, he rode with the others along the creek bank, catching glimpses of the rising moon as they came to wide places where the soft silver light gleamed on the slow-moving water of the stream.

This was, Johnny knew, a shortcut that would bring them to the glade as certainly as the road would have done. He checked his knives in his sleeves, the handgun at his belt, the rifle in its boot.

Now was the time, and he felt his pulse quicken as they drew nearer and nearer to his old enemy. Perhaps the man's blood would wipe out the pain of his loss.

CHAPTER THIRTY

The glade slanted across the road, most of its area lying to the north and east of the track. Some tornado or forest fire had long ago destroyed the trees there, and only saplings and brush had had the time to grow back into the clearing.

The light of the moon, almost at the full, seemed terribly bright after the midnight reaches of the wood. As Johnny and his people neared the place, they passed through lanes of huckleberry and hawthorn to reach the spot Jorge chose as their position.

The soldiers had not arrived as yet, though there was in the distance the faint sound of hooves on dust. From time to time harness clinked or a horse snorted. At last, one of the approaching mounts whinnied, but before any of their own could whinny in reply, the ambushers were holding the beasts' muzzles. Silence filled the moonlit space.

The first horse came into view out of the dense shadow of the trees; a big gray, it shone like silver in the tenuous light. That was the Captain's horse. Johnny had his agents ask and watch and notice everything on their trips into town.

The rider of that horse was no fool. He paused and stared along the road behind and before him. He listened hard, but only the mournful cooing of a dove and the call of a whippoorwill from the forest could be heard amid the ratcheting of crickets and tree frogs. After a long moment, he lifted his hand and the small troop of cavalry followed him into the light, six horses, in column of twos.

The Captain's contempt for mountebanks had evidently not been sufficiently countered.

When the column was strung along the roadway, well clear of the shadow behind them, Senaqua lifted his hand. An uncanny ululation filled the air, yip-yip-yipping in a shattering din across the natural sounds of the night.

With the first note, Johnny's horse burst from the trees, followed by the other stolen mounts. The roar of Ma's shotgun mingled with the crack and snap of rifles and handguns, and four of the riders in the moonlight went down. The rest spurred for the forest beyond the glade, where cover was nearest.

The Captain, however, turned his gray to face the charge. He shouted, and the troopers reined in and moved back to join him in a clump. Bad tactics, Johnny thought, as he swept his riders around the tight knot of men and horses.

Shots picked off two more of the cavalrymen, though Johnny felt more than one slug go zinging past his ears or lift his hair as it passed too near for comfort. Someone fell, and he swung out so that the circle of attackers would not tread on the fallen guerrilla.

A dark-painted rider rode into the remaining cavalry, taking down a horse and a rider together, and Johnny knocked the last trooper off his horse with the butt of his pistol. That left the Captain alone in the clearing, and Ma Devinney, frightening in her Indian getup, came quietly behind the officer and jammed her shotgun barrel into his back.

"You got enough?" she yelled.

The pistol went down and dropped onto the ground. The Captain raised both hands shoulder high and stared about at his strange captors.

"Do any of you savages speak English?" he asked, his eyes glinting pale in the soft light.

"I speak your tongue," said Senaqua. He cocked his head toward Johnny and rode forward. He was bare to the waist, his long hair flowing over his shoulders beneath his headband. No vestige of Hashi Ben Ali remained as he faced the Captain.

"All of us speak your tongue, indeed. You are in our custody, to be punished for your crimes. I hope..."—Senaqua's voice was stern—"...that you understand what those crimes have been and where you committed them."

The man's head was high, his thin nose pinched. "I have done nothing wrong." His hand was too near his rifle boot, and Mugual appeared out of no place and removed it from temptation.

The Captain jerked and held his hands high as the young Comanche removed his ammunition and his other revolver, as well as his saber. "Who claims that I have committed any crime?" he demanded.

Johnny heeled his horse forward into the full glare of the moon. "I do. You hanged my entire family and shot me, although we were no threat to anyone and had taken no part in your stupid war. You left me for dead and my cousin clinging to hold me from falling to my death."

"I have never seen you before in my life!"

Johnny drew nearer and skinned back his sleeve. The moonlight winked dully in the eyes of the small gems of his wristband.

"You do not recognize that? I should think that you would, for you have seen it twice before. I showed it to you first after we destroyed your command in Arkansas. Just my little girl cousin and I, wounded almost to death, accomplished that."

The man jerked almost imperceptibly. The knowledge of who these must be, at least in part, was in his eyes.

"And once I showed this to you in the night, in the north of this territory. You were camped along a creek, and we tied you to a tree and left you." Johnny chuckled.

"The mountebank!" The words were more of a gasp than an exclamation.

Magda dismounted and came to stand beside Johnny's stirrup. "Yes. Both of us. We watched you hang our parents and destroy our world, for no reason. Did you think that we would not care? Do you believe that we feel less for our own people than do those who come from other sorts of lives and professions?"

The man's face was even paler than the silver light might have explained. No one looking at him could doubt that he recalled the hanging that Magda mentioned.

"You have ruined my career! Isn't that enough vengeance? I should have been given a significant command after my service in the War. It had been promised to me, and I would have had my promotion, if I had not had bad luck!" He glanced about wildly. "What is it that you want from me?"

A groan rose from the grass. Ma was off at once, kneeling beside a fallen trooper. "Come and help me," she called to Magda. "And yell for Manuela. This boy is hurt bad, and she needs to bring the medical bag. You can palaver with these idiots later."

"Hold him here," Johnny said to Mugual. He dismounted and moved from body to body, checking for signs of life. Only two of the cavalrymen survived, and the second was dying, as Johnny could see from the blood gushing from a severed artery in his leg. The other would soon die, if nothing was done.

"Come here," he called to the Captain. The officer got down stiffly and came to crouch beside Johnny. "What do you want?" he asked.

"I want you to see what you have done. I want you to understand why you are going to die. You must know both *why* you are to die and how just your death will be. I cannot live in a world where you continue to draw breath."

Johnny stared down at the youngster lying in the grass. His cap had fallen off, and he looked like a child, gasping, eyes closed. It was plain that those eyes would never open again in life.

"This man was under your command. Do you feel anything for him? Any regret at his death or pity for his survivors?" Johnny demanded.

The Captain stared down at the shadowy body. "He did his duty," he said, his tone noncommittal. "That is all a man can do. He was not a very good soldier, but he was learning. Now he will be saved the trouble. Do you expect me to grieve for him?" He sounded genuinely curious.

The boy gave a long sigh, exhaling, and he did not breathe again.

"I tried your way," Johnny said. "I turned off my human emotions, though that is not easy for an Italian to do. I killed men, without thinking of it or looking back at the acts. I did not consider them human beings, but dangers or obstacles.

"I killed a man in a manner that you probably could not imagine, and my heart was cold as chilled shot inside me as I did it. When I think of that death, I become sick to my soul, and I want to cut out that part of me and throw it away, forgetting about it forever. But I will never be able to do that."

He looked up as Magda came to stand beside him. "The other boy is doing fairly well," she said. "How is this...oh. I see." She glared at the Captain but said no more.

"If we killed your mother, led her to a tree and strung a noose about her neck, pulled her up, kicking and gurgling, to strangle, how would you feel about that?" Johnny asked. His voice was so quiet that the small breeze almost smothered the sound of it.

The Captain stood with a convulsive jerk. "My mother is a lady. Educated, refined, beyond reproach. That sort of thing could never happen to her."

Johnny faced him, his teeth clenched for a moment before he could speak. "My mother's family performed for kings and queens in Europe. My mother spoke three languages and could comport herself with the grace of a queen. She was warm and loving to all who had need of her, and because she was who and what she was, you murdered her. Birth and attainments are no protection against the acts of villains."

Magda had come nearer as he spoke, her hands clenched at her sides. Her moonlit eyes said more than her tongue could have done.

The Captain stepped back as she moved toward him. "We are the Steffingtons of New Hampshire," he said. "Such things do not happen to us!"

"If I'm not mightily mistaken," came a gruff voice behind him, "such a thing is about to happen right now, Steffington or not. Right, Johnny?" Ma came to stand beside the girl.

Now the others, finished with tending the wounded man, gathered in a circle around the condemned officer. Even Manuela, too timid to take part in the attack, was there beside her father, clinging to his hand like a small child.

"If all are agreed," said Gian-Carlo Gannelli, "I will hang him now."

"You will be hunted down and hanged in your turn," said the Captain. But his tone did not hold much hope.

"Perhaps. But we gave our words that the one who killed our families would die. If we hang, it will be with our word fulfilled and our vows carried out."

Johnny glanced about. The moon was past zenith, its glare coloring the grass and trees beyond with unreal brightness.

Luke crutched forward and said, "This is just."

Napier, behind him, nodded, his face wild beneath its layer of ash and blood from the crease that had brought him down during the fight.

The two Comanche did not speak, but both watched with dark and enigmatic eyes.

Absalom looked long at the officer, sighed, and nodded.

Hassie Mae, now beside Ma, snorted. "He should have hung long ago, from the way the people in town say he treated them," she said.

Johnny turned to Jorge, whose daughter still clung to his hand. "And you, my friend, what do you say?"

"I have listened as you spoke. I have heard what those in the town had to say, from the mouths of these our friends. I say hang him. Manuela will agree."

* * * * * * *

They led Captain Steffington to the wood and tossed a rope-end over a branch. Absalom came forward to tie the complex knot, which he did with a hangman's skill. "Seen a lot of them made, in my day," he said as he stepped back.

Johnny faced the Captain as he placed the noose about his neck. "You should be grateful that you came into my hands now instead of earlier," he said into the staring eyes.

"I would have tortured you for hours, peeled your eyelids, done things that even the Comanche found hard to believe, if I had caught you a few months ago. But I have come to my senses and am no longer the man I was for a time. I have learned that I cannot remain cruel. It comes back to torture me as keenly as I tortured that brutal man I killed. So I will not pull you up to strangle.

"Mount your horse."

Mugual led the gray forward. The beast snorted and danced, smelling fear on his rider. But when Steffington spoke soothingly, the gelding stood.

In the dapples of moonlight filtering through the branches overhead, Johnny saw the man's eyes darting from right to left, seeking some way out of his predicament, help from some unknown source. But the wood was shrilling with its night cries of insects and birds and beasts, and no sound of man or horse came on the breeze.

Steffington set a foot in the stirrup, paused, and stared at Johnny. His mouth opened, closed, firmly. He mounted, settling himself into the saddle. "I shall see you in Hell," he said, as Johnny drew back his hand to slap the gray's rump.

"At least you understand that is where you are going," said Gannelli, and his hand came down with a crack.

The gray leaped forward, and the snap of the man's neck sounded like a broken branch in the wood.

AFTERWORD

They left the body dangling from the tree. Perhaps searchers would find it, there in the fringe of the wood. Buzzards might lead others to the spot. But they wasted no time in burying him, though they did bury the dead troopers and carried the single living one to a farm, where he would be tended well. He had been unconscious all the while they executed the Captain, so he could tell his fellow soldiers nothing except that they had been attacked by Indians.

Then they moved east through the forest into the flatter, swampier country. Their circus played in Natchitoches, in Lafayette, and then they headed toward New Orleans, hoping to play in that city. There would be a good chance, they thought, of making enough to see them through the winter.

Not one of them could have been recognized as the person he or she had been as little as a year before. Napier felt secure, Johnny saw, even returning to the city governed by Butler's people. Who would look for a gambler under the top-hat of a ringmaster? The mustache changed his appearance incredibly.

Johnny and Magda knew that with Steffington dead it would be unlikely anyone would search for them further, and they were totally unconnected with his death, as far as their former identities were concerned. Nobody who had met them in battle survived to describe them.

The others had nothing to fear from the law, and they flung themselves into their work with great energy. The circus shaped up well. That first flawed and amateurish performance had, even then, promised well for their future. Now they had worked up a smooth and professional show.

Props and equipment were procured or their materials found, and they were constructed along the way. Even the trapeze act was coming together again. Though Johnny's leg was now too stiff for flying, Mugual filled that gap with enthusiasm, and Johnny became catcher. With three in the act they could attempt tricks impossible for a pair of flyers.

Manuela's Spanish dancing became an attraction, as well, for her style was unfamiliar here. Her bright beauty, her shy manner, and her quicksilver feet brought her much acclaim.

Eventually, Johnny knew, some young man would rob them of her services. One such had already followed them halfway across Louisiana, sending her flowers after each evening's show. Both Jorge and Johnny knew the girl was warming to the young fellow's advances. But they would find another dancer, they knew, leaving her secure and well loved with a home of her own.

The rest were busy learning new skills, exerting themselves to the fullest. Nobody thought, any longer, about murder and sudden death. Vendetta was a thing they had left behind, back in that moonlit forest and that awful glade. The death of Steffington seemed to have purged them all of the need for vengeance.

Most surprising of all, Johnny and his cousin agreed, was the manner in which the Comanche had taken to life on the road. Senaqua, with his quiet dignity and his commanding voice rolling out German poetry, was becoming a legend. Lines of people were often waiting to consult him by the time the show reached a new town. From some esoteric Comanche source, he seemed to have a gift for sizing up people and foretelling their fates.

Luke and Hassie Mae came, along the way, to a wordless agreement. At one stop, they found a minister who married them. It changed little in their attitude toward each other, seemingly, or their fellows. With Ma, they formed a sort of nuclear family, about which the rest of the troupe clustered.

Johnny and Magda lived as they had done most of their lives, feeling at times as if the months of flight and danger must have been a dream. But Johnny sometimes had nightmares in which a lidless pair of eyes pleaded with him for mercy, and Magda knew, when he fell silent and morose, that his old deed was haunting him.

The two worked themselves hard, and they pushed toward bigger and better flying, as well as more dangerous knife-throwing tricks. If Johnny thought, as they came bounding into the ring to the music of their accordionist, of Mama and her accordion, of Papa Gannelli and his violin, or of Celie with her steely arabesque, and Barnabas and his iron strength, he said nothing.

They had won their small, intensive war. He had conquered his enemies, without and within, and it was time to live again and to learn the ways of peace once more.

ABOUT THE AUTHOR

The author of seventy books, more than forty of them published commercially, **ARDATH MAYHAR** began her career in the early eighties with science fiction novels from Doubleday and TSR. Atheneum published several of her young adult and children's novels. Changing focus, she wrote westerns (as **Frank Cannon**) and mountain man novels (as **John Killdeer**), four prehistoric Indian books under her own name, and historical western *High Mountain Winter* under the byline **Frances Hurst**.

Recently she has been working with on-line publishers. *A Road of Stars* was her first original novel to appear in print-on-demand format. Many of her out-of-print titles are now available from e-publishers fictionwise.com and renebooks.com; many other novels are being published by the Borgo Press Imprint of Wildside Press and Amazon.com.

Now in her seventies, Mayhar was widowed in 1999, after forty-one years of marriage, and has four grown sons. She now works at home, writing short fiction and nonfiction, and doing book doctoring professionally. Her web pages can be found at:

w2.netdot.com/ardathm/ and
http://ofearna.us/ books/mayhar.html